**"Are you afraid of** ~~me?~~ **demanded as h**~~e~~ **his arms**

"No," Andie whisp~~ered~~ ~~I'm~~ nervous." If only she ~~could learn~~ to enjoy Ben without becoming ~~emotionally~~ involved, without giving up too m~~uch of~~ herself as she'd always done with her family. If only she could trust herself not to fall in love with him.

Ben kissed her thoroughly, again and again, until both of them were gasping for breath. Then he dragged his lips across her cheek to her ear, and down to her throat... tasting, nibbling, making shivers of desire course through her. His hands were as busy as his mouth, exploring, shaping, caressing, until she was arching eagerly against him, starving for more.

"Andie." His voice was hoarse in her ear, his breath hot against her skin. "If you want me to stop, tell me now."

The choice was hers. Play it safe—as she had done all her life—or give in to reckless impulsive pleasure.

Dear Reader

What better way to brighten up the long, dark winter months than by reading an exciting Temptation novel, especially when Temptation has caught the festive spirit with its bright new raspberry-coloured covers.

This will be our new look for 1995—the year when Temptation gets to celebrate its 10th Anniversary!—so step into Christmas and the New Year with even more passionate, fun-loving stories from Temptation. We know you'll enjoy the good reading we have lined up for you in the year ahead.

The Editor
Mills & Boon Temptation
Eton House
18-24 Paradise Road
Richmond
Surrey TW9 1SR

# *Just Her Luck*

## GINA WILKINS

MILLS & BOON LIMITED
ETON HOUSE, 18-24 PARADISE ROAD
RICHMOND, SURREY TW9 1SR

All the characters in this book have no existence outside the imagination of the author, and have no relation whatsoever to anyone bearing
the same name or names. They are not even distantly inspired by any
individual known or unknown to the author, and all the incidents are
pure invention.

MILLS & BOON and the Rose Device are trademarks of the
publisher. TEMPTATION is a trademark of Harlequin Enterprises
Limited, used under licence.

First published in Great Britain in 1994
by Mills & Boon Limited, Eton House, 18-24 Paradise Road,
Richmond, Surrey TW9 1SR

© Gina Wilkins 1994

ISBN 0 263 79005 3

21 - 9412

Printed in Great Britain by
BPC Paperbacks Ltd

# Prologue

"YOU WOULDN'T MIND doing just this one little favor for your mother, would you, Benji?"

"Mother, I've asked you not to call me that. It makes me feel like a small furry dog." Benjamin Luck shifted the telephone to his other ear and reached for the cup of coffee sitting in front of him on his breakfast table. The thought of how much trouble doing his mother a "little favor" usually turned out to be made him wish the coffee was a more potent beverage. Something told him he was going to need a stiff drink before this call was finished.

"Sorry, darling. I'll try to remember. But about this little favor . . ." she said, returning to the reason for her long-distance call to Ben's apartment in Portland, Oregon.

"*Little* favor?" Ben repeated incredulously. "You want me to take an indeterminate length of time off work and go haring off around the country looking for your loony friend's runaway daughter. A daughter, I might add, who is over twenty-one and has every right to run away from home if she wants."

"But, darling, you said you have a bit of spare time now that you've wrapped up your last case. And it's not as if I'm asking something you don't know how to do— you *are* an investigator, after all."

"I'm an insurance-fraud investigator, Mother. That hardly qualifies me to—"

She blithely ignored him, not at all to his surprise. "And you were planning to take a week or so of vacation, weren't you? So it's not as if you don't have the time now."

"A vacation implies doing something I *want* to do— you know, relaxing, having fun, not working?"

"But Andie's family is so worried about her. She's never done anything like this before—quitting her job and running off to 'find' herself. She's always been so responsible, so dependable, so sensible. Everyone thought she'd come home quickly, but it's been almost four months now."

"Look, Mom, I know Gladys McBride has been a friend of yours for a lot of years—"

"Yes, she has."

"But I really don't think that we have any business interfering in her daughter's life," Ben continued firmly. "You said Andie is twenty-five. That's long past the age of majority, and she has every right to do whatever she wants with her life. We have no legal reason to track her down, no justifiable excuse to—"

"There's something I haven't told you, Ben," Jessie cut in again, choosing her words cautiously. "Something a little more serious than Andie just moving away from her family."

Ben swallowed a groan. With Jessie, there was always "something a little more." And it was always a kicker. He still bore a few scars to prove it. "What haven't you told me, Mother?" he asked with a sigh.

She cleared her throat delicately. "You see, there's this psychic . . ."

Ben closed his eyes and groped blindly for his coffee mug. It was only eight o'clock in the morning and he really could use a stiff drink.

# 1

THE WARY TYKE took one look at Andie McBride's bright red nose, painted ear-to-ear grin and rainbow-striped hair and burst into shrieks of pure terror. Since this wasn't an unprecedented reaction, Andie knew how to handle it. She promptly backed up three steps to put a nonthreatening distance between herself and the child, held out a colorful helium balloon in one gloved hand and cooed, "Don't cry, sweetie pie. Would you like a balloon?"

Still blubbering, the little boy looked greedily at the balloon, though his desire for it wasn't quite strong enough to overcome his aversion to the clown. The boy's father—one of those macho, boys-don't-cry types that Andie particularly disliked—gave his son a rough push forward. "It's just a clown, Bobby. Quit being such a sissy and take the balloon."

Andie took another step back, shaking her be-wigged head. "No, don't force him. Here, you take the balloon and then you can give it to him."

"My kid ain't going to be afraid of clowns," the man retorted, pushing the resisting boy forward again.

"He will be if you force him at me now," Andie replied, keeping her distance from the child.

"For Pete's sake, Harold, take the balloon," the child's tired-looking mother ordered her husband crossly. "I'm thirsty and I want to sit down a minute."

"Look, Mommy, a clown! Giving out balloons! Hi, clown. Can I have one?" a little girl in pink bloomers called as she rushed up. She was followed by several siblings in assorted sizes, none of whom suffered from clown phobia. All jostled one another to get as close as possible to Andie.

Somewhat reassured by the other children's enthusiasm, the little boy looked from his scowling father to Andie's bright smile, then tentatively held out a grubby hand for the balloon. She placed the string in his hand, careful to keep her movements slow and easy. "There you go. Hold on tightly now, you don't want it to float away."

"I'll tie it on his arm," his mother said, leading him away. "Thanks," she added over her shoulder.

With a smothered sigh, Andie turned to the crowd of children clamoring around her oversize feet, begging for her attention. "Well, hi, boys and girls! Who wants a balloon?"

"I do! I do!"

Ben munched a candy apple and took grateful advantage of the shade of a towering oak tree as he watched the clown at work several yards away. So this was Andie McBride, he mused, trying to guess what she might look like beneath the wig and greasepaint. He'd seen photographs, of course, but the dark-haired, dark-eyed, sweet-faced young woman in the pictures bore little resemblance to this brightly garbed, bizarrely painted creature. Had he not known who she was, he'd have been hard-pressed to say whether the person disguised by the wig and baggy costume was a woman or a slender young man.

He tugged at the collar of his short-sleeved knit shirt and wondered how Andie managed to look so cool in this blasted mid-July-in-Texas heat. He wasn't wearing nearly as much clothing as she was, and he was sweltering; yet her pancake makeup wasn't even running with perspiration.

He'd been watching her for almost half an hour, trying to decide when to make his move. He had his cover firmly in place, but he wasn't eager to start lying to her. Still, he had to have an excuse for being here. There weren't many thirty-two-year-old males hanging around alone in this circus theme park filled with parents and children.

Maybe he should have given more serious consideration to his mother's improbable suggestion that he borrow a couple of kids for the weekend. Problem was, where would he have found them? Acme Rent-a-Kid? he wondered wryly.

It would have been so much easier just to walk up to her and say that he was the son of a friend of her mother's and had looked her up as a favor to her family to make sure she was okay. But he'd had to swear to his mother, Andie's parents, her sister, her brother-in-law and her grandmother that he wouldn't tell her who he was or who had sent him, which tied his hands considerably.

*Someday, Mother, someone's going to learn how to say no when you ask one of your little favors. I just hope it's me.*

When the mob of children finally moved away from the clown, Ben tossed his apple core into a nearby trash container, ran a hand through his breeze-tossed dark hair and started toward her. Only to be almost run down by a crowd of squealing preschoolers of every shape, size and color, but all wearing identical yellow T-shirts identifying them as belonging to the Smiling Faces Daycare Center. In moments Andie the clown was hidden behind a mass of laughing, shoving, shouting children and their three harried-looking supervisors.

It was going to be a while before she was free again, Ben realized. He swallowed a sigh and decided to treat himself to a cold soft drink before his next attempt to communicate with Andie McBride.

HIS SOCKLESS sneakered feet crossed on the metal railing in front of him, Ben tossed a handful of popcorn into his mouth and idly watched the circus act in the center ring. According to the park information pamphlet, the circus at four o'clock was a daily attraction. He'd arrived in the huge tent early, so he'd gotten a front-row seat. He hadn't been tempted to linger at the noisy carnival booths or crowded rides or tacky gift shops filling the rest of the park.

Five hours in this bizarre park, he thought with a sigh, and he still hadn't found an opportunity to approach Andie. Every time he'd gotten close to her, he'd been pushed aside by a mob of clown-loving ankle biters.

She'd disappeared completely at about two o'clock. Ben had assumed she was taking a lunch break. She hadn't reappeared and had been replaced by another roving clown. This hadn't worried him, since he'd been told she always appeared in the daily circus performance. He'd assumed she would appear as one of the circus clowns.

There were quite a few clowns working the big top this afternoon. None of them, however, was Andie. He decided he might as well watch the rest of the show, since he hadn't a clue where Andie went when she wasn't working. Furthermore he had no mailing address except the post-office-box number she used when corresponding with her grandmother.

He'd seen better circuses, but it seemed to satisfy the under-twelve set. A slightly chubby equestrian was followed by a couple of sluggish trained elephants, a quartet of dancing poodles, a skinny tightrope walker and trapeze artists who elicited a few gasps of amazement, though not from Ben. And then the clowns performed again—the tired old clown-trapped-in-the-burning-building routine.

Ben finished his popcorn and washed it down with the remaining third of his soda. He was starting to feel a bit queasy, maybe because he'd done nothing all day but eat. Thinking back, he realized that he'd had a couple of hot dogs—with peppers and onions—an ear of roasted corn, a candy apple, a powdered-sugar-sprinkled funnel cake, an ice-cream cone, a bag of salt-water taffy, a chunk of macadamia-nut fudge, and the popcorn he'd just finished. He'd lost count of the sodas he'd had with it all.

Maybe he'd better forgo the fresh roasted peanuts an earnest-looking teenager was hawking in the aisle next to him.

Then he spotted Andie McBride again and forgot all about his protesting stomach. Only this time she wasn't dressed like a clown. This time she was hardly dressed at all.

She wore a strapless lavender satin garment no larger than a bathing suit, spangled in sequins and cut high on her thighs to reveal long luscious legs clad in dark stockings. With seams. She balanced effortlessly on the highest, tiniest heels he'd ever seen. Her bare arms were smooth and tanned, the enticing hint of cleavage over her costume creamy and flawless. He wasn't the only man in the audience who suddenly sat up straight and mouthed, "Hot damn!"

Had he not memorized every detail of her photo-graph, he might not have recognized her as the prim-looking woman in the photo. Now her near-black hair was a mass of sexy tousled waves that tumbled about her bare shoulders. Her oval face was dramatically made up to maximize her huge dark eyes and full pouty lips.

Feeling rather as if he'd just been trampled by an elephant, Ben blinked to clear his vision and stared at what was going on in the center ring. Andie was climbing into a long narrow box, apparently eager to be sawn in two by Milo the Magnificent, an aging paunchy little man in a cheap tuxedo.

So this was how Andie McBride, former dental assistant from Seattle, was finding herself. No wonder her stunned family was worried.

Milo wasn't magnificent. Ben had seen all the illusions before, and more impressively performed. But he, like the other adult males in the audience, was more interested in the assistant than the magician, anyway. And he was more determined than ever to introduce himself to her. One way or another, he was going to learn all there was to know about Andie McBride—and his burning curiosity about her suddenly had little, if anything, to do with the favor his mother had requested.

ANDIE CHANGED rapidly out of her sexy magician's-assistant costume after the performance. She laced up her worn tennis shoes with a sigh of relief, delighted, as always, to be free of the murderous spiked heels she wore during the circus act. Then she grabbed her big purple canvas tote, slung it over her shoulder and headed for the dressing-room exit. Her stomach reminded her that she'd skipped lunch to practice a new illusion with Milo; she was starving.

"Hey, Andie. Want to go to a movie or somethin' this evening?" Polly, the bosomy blond equestrian, called from across the communal women's dressing room, where she was changing out of her own sequins and spangles into a tight Western-cut shirt and jeans.

"Thanks, Polly, but I'd better pass. I've got a date with a washer and dryer."

"Laundry? On a Saturday night? Bor-r-r-ring. Only reason I don't have a date is 'cause Junior had to make an unexpected run."

"That happens when you date a trucker," Andie answered sympathetically, although she'd never dated a trucker in her life. "But I've been putting this laundry off for a week now. The situation's getting critical."

"Okay. Some other time then," Polly said good-naturedly.

"You bet. See you Monday." Andie made her escape before Polly could detain her any longer. She liked Polly, but the woman was an avid talker, and Andie was ready to leave. She wanted to eat, run a few errands, then tackle her laundry. Certainly not an exciting schedule, but at least she had no one to answer to but herself once working hours were over. The errands she would run were her own, as were the garments she'd be washing that evening. What a welcome change.

Tugging absently at the hem of her yellow knit sleeveless romper, she stepped out of the main tent and almost straight into the arms of a handsome dark-haired man in khaki shorts and a white knit shirt.

"Watch out!" she said, stumbling to keep from running smack into him.

His hands shot out to catch her shoulders, his palms rough and warm against her bare skin. "Sorry. You okay?"

His voice was deep and rich, his eyes very green, with long sexy lashes. Nice. "Yes, of course." She took two steps back to break the contact between them. "Um . . . this area is for park employees only. Are you lost? Can I give you directions to someplace in particular?"

"You're Andie McBride, aren't you?"

She lifted an eyebrow. "Yes?"

He held out his right hand. "I'm Ben Sherman. Mr. Parker suggested I speak to you."

"Mr. Parker?" Andie parroted, wondering why the park owner would have sent this man to her. "What is it you want, Mr. Sherman?"

"I'm a travel writer," he explained. "I'm doing a series of articles on family vacation spots and the people who work at them. I was hoping you'd give me an interview about what you do here and why you wanted to work in a circus theme park. Maybe add a few humorous anecdotes about your experiences with the tourists and children."

Andie was thoroughly confused. "You want an interview with *me?* But I'm relatively new here. And I'm really not that interesting. I don't know why Mr. Parker suggested me."

"He said you were very personable," Ben explained with a reassuring smile. "And since you work as both a clown and a magician's assistant, I think you're very interesting. I'm sure my readers would, as well."

"It's a small park, Mr. Sherman, with a somewhat limited staff. Several of us work in more than one capacity."

"Please, call me Ben. As I explained, I'll be interviewing several of your coworkers. You certainly don't have to participate of course, if it makes you uncomfortable. I'm sure Mr. Parker would understand."

Andie swallowed a groan. Mr. Parker would *not* understand. She knew he'd do anything to make this park start paying off, to be able to compete with the larger better-known parks such as Six Flags, or even Disneyland. If he thought she made a good spokesperson for his park, he would be terribly displeased if she refused without one heck of a good reason. And she wasn't sure he'd accept the truth—that she'd run away from home at the ripe old age of twenty-five and was reluctant for her loving family to learn her whereabouts.

*Oh, for crying out loud, Andie. Get a backbone. Your family's going to have to find out about this eventually, anyway. Do your job.* "All right, Mr. . . .uh, Ben," she said. "I'd be happy to tell you about my work here. When would you like to interview me?"

"We could start now," he replied with a smile of pleasure at her acceptance. "Unless you have other plans?"

She glanced at her watch. It was almost six. Early for dinner, but not when she hadn't eaten since breakfast. "I missed lunch today and I'm ravenous. Why don't you join me in the staff cafeteria and we can talk over dinner?"

"Dinner," he repeated with a notable lack of enthusiasm. "All right. Thank you."

She eyed him questioningly. "Is something wrong?"

He shook his head, his charming smile returning. "Not at all. Lead the way, Ms. McBride."

THE THEME PARK'S employee dining room made Ben feel as though he'd somehow stepped through a looking glass. The rides, game booths and some sideshows operated until ten at night, Andie had explained, but her shift ended at five with the conclusion of the daily circus performance. After that, most of the participants gathered in the dining room to eat and unwind.

Ben looked at the fried chicken, creamed potatoes and peas on the sectioned plastic plate in front of him and wondered if he'd explode if he ate another bite. The food looked and smelled tempting, though he certainly wasn't hungry. He picked up his fork, figuring a few bites more wouldn't hurt him. Andie was attacking her pot roast and vegetables with delicate greed.

"Tell me a little about yourself," he said casually, when he decided she'd taken the edge off her hunger enough to concentrate on conversation. "How did you end up working at a circus park?"

"Sounds like he wants to know what a nice girl like you is doing in a place like this," a cheerful voice commented.

Ben looked up—and up—and up. The man carrying a tray past their table-for-two had to be several inches over seven feet and might have weighed a hundred and fifty pounds, soaking wet. He was all knees and elbows and protruding ears, but with an infectious smile that made Ben like him instinctively.

Andie glanced up and smiled. "Oh, hi, Milton. This is Ben Sherman, a travel writer doing an article about the park. Be nice to him or you'll have Parker to answer to."

The towering Milton rolled his eyes comically. "Anything but that! You just let me know if there's any way I can be of help to you, Mr. Sherman."

"I'll do that. Maybe you'd give me an interview in the next day or so?" Ben asked, mindful of his cover.

"Of course. Nice to meet you, Sherman. See you around, Andie."

Ben waited until the tall man had moved on before saying, "So, um, what *is* a nice girl like you doing in a place like this?"

Andie smiled and shook her head. "Don't mind Milton. He's never serious. As to what I'm doing here—I like it here. It's as simple as that."

"Hardly," Ben murmured, frustrated by the nonanswer. "This isn't exactly an ordinary job. There had to be something that drew you to it, something more than just liking it here."

"Sure there was. Money. I do get paid, you know."

"Forgive me for being crass, but wouldn't you make a great deal more at a traditional job? A roving clown and magician's assistant in a newly established theme park can't be earning a huge salary."

She shrugged, apparently not offended by his calculated bluntness. "My salary feeds me and pays my few bills. It's all I need—for now."

Ben was tempted to follow up on that "for now," but decided to let it pass for the moment. He was still trying to figure out how Andie had ended up as a clown in Mercury, Texas, after leaving Seattle. "Do you come from a circus family? Are you following in the footsteps of several generations of clowns or performers?" he asked, hoping the improbable suggestions would encourage her to discuss her family with him.

Before she could answer, another voice interrupted. "Hi, Andie. Good show today. Milo was in great form, wasn't he?" A hefty bald man waddled past the table as he spoke. Two teacup poodles grinned out at Ben from the patch pockets on the front of the man's shabby tweed jacket. Ben stared at them.

Andie smiled brightly. "Thanks, Kirby. Yes, he was. I was very proud of him. Milo works so hard at his illusions."

Two demanding yips drew her attention to Kirby's bulging pockets. "Hi, Ping. Hello, Pong. How are you boys today?"

Two eager barks answered her. Kirby nodded pleasantly at Ben and kept moving, murmuring to the poodles as he departed.

*Twilight Zone*, Ben thought, resisting an impulse to shake his head and rub his eyes. *You owe me for this, Mother.*

Andie turned back to Ben and answered his question as though they'd never been interrupted. "No, I'm not from a circus family. I had a typical middle-class upbringing. My family's quite average actually."

Ben took a hasty swallow of iced tea to disguise a snort of disbelief. The McBride family, average? Hardly.

He still shuddered every time he remembered the family conference at which he'd been briefed on Andie's mysterious departure. Her mother, Gladys, had wrung her hands and loudly bewailed Andie's disloyalty. She'd even quoted Shakespeare—that line about how sharper than a serpant's tooth to have a thankless child. She must have said it half a dozen times, until her own mother, Maybelle, who'd come from her nursing home to join the conference, had finally told Gladys to "put a sock in it."

Donald Humphries, Andie's brother-in-law and former employer, had insisted with stuffy confidence that Andie had suffered a nervous breakdown and was in desperate need of psychiatric counseling. Why else, he'd demanded arrogantly, would she have broken up with a fine young man from an excellent family and a promising career in his dental office to run away and join the circus?

Donald's wife, Gloria, Andie's older sister, had seemed convinced that Andie should be kidnapped and deprogrammed. She'd seen a discussion of that process on "Geraldo," she'd said earnestly, and Andie had all the symptoms of a person who'd been brainwashed. Did Ben know any professional deprogrammers? One who could work quickly? They all wanted Andie back exactly the way she'd been before this unfortunate situation.

Dr. Nolan McBride, Andie's ancient-history-professor father, had appeared to be in an intellectual daze throughout most of the conference. He'd actually had to be reminded on more than one occasion of the purpose for the family meeting. "Oh, yes," he'd murmured. "My missing daughter, Andrea. When you find her, young man, please be so kind as to ask her where she put my notes on the Peloponnesian War."

Only Andie's grandmother, Maybelle Canfield, had seemed in any way rational, as far as Ben had been concerned. She was a voice of sanity in the chaos, silencing the others with a few choice words when they got completely out of hand. She was the only one in the family who'd known Andie had been planning to leave, the only one with whom Andie had kept in touch during the past three months. She was convinced Andie had every right to make her own choices, and she'd known exactly where her granddaughter was, though she'd had only a post-office box rather than a complete address. But even she was growing concerned about "this psychic business," she'd said soberly.

"Andie's too gullible," she'd murmured to Ben, out of hearing of the others. "Not because of a lack of intelligence, but because of an overly soft heart. As hard as she tries, she still has trouble saying no to anyone who claims to need her help. I was glad when she finally walked out on this family, who have been using her for too many years, but now I'm afraid she's gotten herself into an even worse mess. I don't want her dragged back here, Benjamin. I just want you to make sure she's all right."

It was too soon to tell for sure, of course, but Andie looked perfectly all right to Ben. In fact, she looked terrific; beautiful, healthy and perfectly content with her job and her new friends. Okay, so employment in a circus park in Texas was a radical change from living at home in Seattle and working as a dental assistant. But Ben didn't see any reason to be concerned. Hell, he'd rather entertain kids than clean teeth himself. Any day.

A raucous burst of laughter from a group of clowns at a corner table brought him abruptly back to the present. Andie was studying him covertly as she finished her meal. Ben became aware that he'd drifted into his own thoughts about her family and the conversation had lagged for several long minutes.

He cleared his throat and prepared to continue the farce of interviewing her, though the deception was becoming more distasteful with each passing moment.

# 2

His travel-writer cover in mind, Ben carefully phrased his next question. "How did you—" he began, only to be interrupted once more, this time by two dark-haired well-built young men in white leotards. Ben recognized them as trapeze artists from the circus performance. He tensed a bit when they swooped down on Andie with hugs and kisses, then relaxed when one of them giggled and they strolled off arm in arm.

Now why had he suddenly found himself resenting another man's hands on Andie McBride's shoulders? Maybe, he thought ruefully, it was because he'd been fighting a growing urge to get his own hands on her. Ever since he'd seen her shimmering in the spotlights, lithe and slim and infinitely desirable in skintight satin and sexier-than-hell dark stockings and heels, he'd had to work much too hard to keep his reactions to her distant and professional. And he hadn't been entirely successful.

Andie looked at him in apology when the trapeze artists left them. "I guess this wasn't such a good idea. We'll never be able to talk here without interruption. Sorry."

"I would like a chance to talk to you in more depth," Ben said, taking immediate advantage of the opening.

"Find out how you learned about this place, what qualifications you needed to be hired, how you trained for your duties. Some of the situations you've encountered since you started working here."

*And how have you been spending your time when you aren't working? Is there some man who's been entertaining you when you've finished entertaining others, Andie McBride?*

He prudently kept these last two questions to himself, though he had every intention of discovering the answers before he left Texas. He told himself he was only doing the job he'd been assigned, giving it the same thorough attention he gave all his assignments. *Yeah. Sure.*

Andie didn't look particularly enthused by his list of questions, but she was obviously making every effort to cooperate. Ben wasn't surprised that Andie didn't want to displease her employer. Parker was a fire-eater—and not the kind who performed in sideshows.

"Would you like to schedule another interview in a quieter place?" she offered.

Ben could think of several places he wouldn't mind taking her. Her place. His hotel room. *Any* hotel room. "Wherever you like," he said blandly.

She looked undecided for a moment, then suggested tentatively, "I suppose we could do it at my place . . ."

He managed not to groan at her inadvertently provocative wording.

"My housemate won't bother us during the interview," she added.

Housemate? Not exactly what he'd had in mind. "Your housemate works here, too?" He wanted very badly to ask if the housemate was male or female, but decided to find out a bit more subtly than that.

"Yes."

"Another clown?"

"No. She's a psychic. She works the fortune-teller's tent on the midway."

*The psychic.* Ben's eyebrow lifted. "Sounds like someone I should interview for my article."

"No," Andie said, just a bit too quickly. "I don't think she'll want to be interviewed. She's, um a bit shy about publicity."

Ben was immediately suspicious. So the psychic didn't care for publicity, hmm? He wondered what she was trying to hide.

"She's really very— Oh, here she is now," Andie said, gesturing toward someone approaching from behind him.

Ben looked around with interest, then fought to keep his surprise from showing on his face. *This* was Andie's housemate?

The woman who looked to be in her late fifties had neat silver hair, oddly luminous violet eyes, a gently lined face, and a comfortably rounded figure. She wore a floating purple thing and a glittering pin in the shape of a bird—a hawk, he thought, or maybe a raven. Hard to tell.

"Rosalyn, I'd like you to meet Ben Sherman. He's a travel writer, doing an article about our park. Ben, this is Rosalyn Carmody. My housemate."

Funny, he hadn't imagined the psychic who had everyone so worried would look like someone's grandmother. "Er, nice to meet you, Mrs. Carmody," he murmured, rising belatedly to gesture toward an empty chair at their table. "Please join us."

"I'd love to, but I haven't the time," Rosalyn replied in a soothing melodious voice that Ben figured must come in handy in her profession. "I'm on a break from my shift, and I must be getting back to my tent." She looked at Ben with a rather disconcerting intensity. "Ben Sherman, did you say?"

"Yes, ma'am," he replied, hiding a smile at the thought of lying to a psychic. "I'm interviewing Andie about her work here. Perhaps you could find a moment to talk to me during the next day or so?"

Ben noted the way Rosalyn's eyes met Andie's for a meaningful moment before she answered him. "I'd be delighted," she said, extending a hand as though to seal the deal.

A bit surprised at the gesture and the acceptance, Ben took her hand in his. Her grip tightened and she did not immediately withdraw her hand. Her violet eyes never wavered from his face, and he fought the impulse to shuffle his feet or look away.

"Yes," she said at length, drawing the word out thoughtfully. "I'll talk to you, Mr., um, Sherman. I'd like to know exactly what it is you're after. For your article of course," she added with a sweet smile, pulling her hand from his.

Ben did not believe in psychics or mind readers or mediums or any other new age garbage. There was no way this woman could touch his hand and know that everything he'd just told her had been a lie, including his surname. "Of course," he said smoothly, shoving his strangely tingling hand into his pocket. "Whenever it's convenient for you."

"Andie can tell you where to find my tent. Come by anytime. Andie, I'll see you this evening. Have a nice time—and don't take everything at face value," Rosalyn murmured with a mischievous smile that took twenty years off her age.

Ben stared after the older woman as she floated away. What the hell? He noticed she was joined at the door of the dining hall by Milo the Magnificent. Their heads were close together as they left.

He turned back to Andie to find her watching him with outright suspicion. "What?" he asked.

"You're sure you only want to interview me for an article? You've been completely honest with me from the first?"

Ben didn't even blink. "I told you Mr. Parker gave me permission for this article. You're welcome to call him for confirmation."

"Rosalyn seemed to think you're hiding something."

He lifted an eyebrow. "Her psychic abilities, I suppose?"

"Don't make fun of her. I happen to be very fond of her. And she *does* have psychic abilities. She's no fraud."

He couldn't hide his skepticism and didn't even try. But he was starting to get worried now. Maybe Andie's family *had* been right in their eccentrically misguided manner. Maybe there *was* something going on here. Apparently Madame Rosalyn had Andie completely snowed. "Whatever you say."

"You don't believe me."

"I don't believe in psychics."

She surprised him with a chuckle. "Neither did I before I met Rosalyn. You may have a few surprises in store for you, Mr. Sherman."

"I'm counting on it, Ms. McBride," he couldn't resist murmuring in return.

Her smile faded. She cleared her throat. "So," she said, all business again, "when would you like to try again with the interview?"

"Tonight? Your place?"

"I'm afraid not. I have things to do tonight."

"Tomorrow, then? Do you work on Sundays?"

"Yes, but only till two o'clock. The circus doesn't perform on Sundays."

"Then why don't I meet you outside your dressing room at two, and we'll take it from there?"

"Fine."

"Great." He wasn't completely satisfied, but told himself to take it easy. Rushing her at this point, particularly after the flaky psychic had spooked her, would be a grave mistake. "See you tomorrow, Andie."

She nodded. "Tomorrow."

He watched her walk away. Great legs, he thought again, admiring the way they flashed beneath the hem of her short swingy romper.

*Just what have you gotten yourself into, Andie McBride?*

And what had he gotten himself into by agreeing to help her family?

ANDIE NEVER HAD REASON to believe she was being followed after she left the park.

An old Lynyrd Skynyrd tape provided diversion as Ben waited patiently behind the wheel of his car outside the small redbrick post office located in Mercury's town square. Ben had found an inconspicuous spot only a few yards from Andie's car after she'd dashed inside the building. She emerged before long with a stack of white envelopes, which she tossed into the passenger seat of her battered economy car before driving away.

Ben hummed along with the tape as he followed her through the town. It was an inviting little place, but he wondered why Parker had chosen to establish his amusement park near such a remote, hardly-on-the-map town.

The Big Top Park was about an hour and a half out of Dallas, which put it in perilous competition with Arlington's popular Six Flags over Texas. Considering the lack of tourist facilities offered in the Mercury area, Ben didn't give Parker's enterprise much of a chance for long-term success. But, hey, he thought, negotiating a sharp turn to keep Andie in sight, stranger things had happened.

Andie spent ten minutes in a pharmacy and then another half an hour in a Piggly Wiggly grocery store. Ben sat in the parking lot, exchanged the Lynyrd Skynyrd tape for one by the Allman Brothers and tapped out the rhythm on his steering wheel. He was rewarded for his patience when Andie's final stop was outside a tidy little frame house on the outskirts of town. He parked down the street and watched as she balanced her parcels and fumbled for her door key.

Pleased with his success at learning her home address, Ben eased his purposefully nondescript sedan into gear and drove away. He decided to be content with what he'd accomplished for that day. Besides, he thought ruefully, he could use some bicarb. Maybe he'd make a stop at that pharmacy himself.

ANDIE FOLDED her last clean pair of panties, and put them away, then gave a sigh of weary relief and dropped into a chair. The laundry was done, the bills paid, her weekly letter to her grandmother written, addressed and stamped to be mailed the next day. There was nothing left to do this evening.

Which gave her plenty of time to think about Ben Sherman.

She was still trying to analyze her reactions to him. Attraction, yes, but that wasn't so surprising. Ben was a very attractive man. Any normal woman would have noticed.

But there'd been something else. Something about the way he'd looked at her. About the way he'd smiled at her. About the way she'd felt when their eyes had met across the table. Something that had left her feeling a bit . . . restless. Unsettled. Itchy.

She shook her head in self-disgust. Honestly, she thought, she was acting like a silly teenager. Okay, so he was a good-looking man with a sexy walk and a killer smile. She could appreciate those attributes without making a fool of herself. Though she'd found herself instinctively liking him, there was something about Ben Sherman she didn't quite trust.

She'd been aware of the niggling doubt even before Rosalyn had sent her that obscure warning about not taking everything at face value. Andie didn't think Ben was dangerous exactly, unless one counted that smile of his. Rosalyn hadn't seemed particularly concerned about him. Just wary.

Rosalyn. Andie looked down at her watch with a sudden frown. She gasped when she realized it was well after eleven. Where was she? The park had closed at ten; Rosalyn should have been home more than half an hour ago.

Andie pulled her lower lip between her teeth and began to pace.

Half an hour wasn't very late, she reminded herself, trying to stay calm. But what if something had happened? What if Rosalyn's location had been discovered again? What if she'd been grabbed... or... or worse? Andie shuddered at the possibilities created by her overactive imagination.

She heard the front door open and sighed in relief. From the doorway of her bedroom, she watched her housemate enter the hallway. "You're in late tonight, aren't you?" she said, trying not to sound scolding. "I was beginning to worry."

"I am a bit late," Rosalyn agreed apologetically. "Milo took me out for a drink after closing. I'm sorry I worried you— I should have called."

"Don't be silly," Andie said, suddenly feeling foolish. "You certainly don't have to report in to me when you want to go for a drink with a friend. It's just that I... " She paused, not wanting to bring up the unpleasant topic they rarely discussed.

Rosalyn nodded. "I know, dear. You're concerned about me. And I appreciate it. But you shouldn't worry about the mess I've managed to get myself into. You're too young to waste so much time worrying," she added with an indulgent smile.

Andie shrugged lightly, knowing she wouldn't stop being concerned about her housemate. She had grown very fond of the older woman, who reminded her in some ways of her beloved grandmother. The first time they'd met, Rosalyn had taken Andie's hand and told her she was fulfilling her destiny by coming to Big Top.

She'd hinted that Andie would gain even more than she'd hoped for when she'd started out on her quest to find herself.

Andie had been skeptical at first. But it hadn't taken her long to realize that Rosalyn was no fraud. Though Andie couldn't explain it, she'd grown to accept that Rosalyn had a gift that defied logic.

The knowledge that someone had been stalking Rosalyn for two years—and intended to kill her if he found her—had been giving Andie nightmares ever since Rosalyn had confided in her several weeks ago. Rosalyn had been reluctant to burden Andie with her troubles, but had felt it only fair to warn her that sharing a house with her could prove risky. That hadn't discouraged Andie of course; it had only made her all the more certain that Rosalyn needed someone to look out for her.

She was secretly delighted with the reason for Rosalyn's tardiness this evening. It was the second time this week that Rosalyn had gone out with Milo. Andie had been all but pushing Milo and Rosalyn into each other's arms since she'd met them. Both were middle-aged and lonely, and Andie thought they'd make a terrific couple. "So you were with Milo, were you?" she asked encouragingly.

"It was just a drink, Andie," Rosalyn said with an exasperated shake of her silvery head, well aware of Andie's matchmaking efforts.

"Oh, I'm sure it was," Andie said with a sigh. "You certainly haven't encouraged poor Milo to expect anything more."

Rosalyn's violet eyes turned grave. "Andie, I know you mean well, but you have to understand that I can't risk getting anyone else mixed up with my troubles. I shouldn't even have told you about them."

"Yes, you should have," Andie said flatly. "I'm your friend and I want to help you."

Rosalyn shook her head sadly. "I'm not sure anyone can help me," she murmured, then changed the subject before Andie could pursue the argument. "How was your dinner with Mr. Sherman?"

"I'm afraid we didn't get much accomplished for his article," Andie admitted. "We kept getting interrupted. I guess the staff dining room wasn't the best choice, but I was too hungry to think clearly when I suggested it."

"A travel writer, is he?"

"That's what he said." Andie studied her friend's face intently. "Do you have reason to believe he isn't?"

Rosalyn raised her delicate eyebrows in an innocent expression that Andie had long since learned to suspect. "Why should he lie about something like that?"

"You tell me."

Rosalyn laughed and patted Andie's arm. "I really have nothing else to tell you. I spent only a few minutes with him."

"But what about that warning you gave me about not taking things at face value? What did you mean? And why did you tell him you'd give him an interview when we both know how important it is for you to avoid publicity?"

"I was only suggesting that there may be more to your Mr. Sherman than a pretty face and charming smile. As for the interview—I think I can answer a few of his questions without putting myself in peril."

"He's not *my* Mr. Sherman," Andie muttered, suspecting that Rosalyn knew something she wasn't willing to share at the moment.

Rosalyn laughed again, then said, "I'm tired, dear. I believe I'll turn in. Sleep well."

"Rosalyn," Andie wailed when her housemate moved away.

Rosalyn glanced back from the doorway of her bedroom. "Send him to my tent tomorrow. I'll talk to him. If I sense anything I think you should know, I'll tell you."

Somewhat mollified, Andie nodded. She assumed that Rosalyn must know what she was doing. "All right. Good night."

Andie was still thinking about Ben Sherman when she drifted to sleep that night. Her last clear mental image was of a pair of wicked emerald eyes that held temptation and secrets.

ON SUNDAY MORNING after showering and dressing in denim cutoffs and a striped T-shirt, Ben placed a long-distance telephone call. A deep male voice answered on the other end.

"Hi, Jon. It's Ben."

The laugh that came through the receiver was a mocking one. "Don't tell me you're having trouble doing another one of Mom's little favors."

"I'm handling it," Ben returned with a scowl, guiltily remembering the way he'd laughed at Jon the time he'd been in the same situation. "By the way, how's Amanda?" he asked, thinking of the outcome of Jon's mission of mercy a year earlier.

Jon, a Seattle homicide cop, had been "volunteered" to protect the orphaned grandson of one of Jessie's friends from a would-be kidnapper. At some point during that assignment, Jon had fallen in love with the boy's aunt. He had married her and was now living contentedly in Seattle with Amanda and her endearingly brilliant young nephew, A.J., who'd quickly become a favorite in the Luck family.

"Amanda's doing great," Jon said proudly. "The doctor says she's in perfect health, and so is the baby. I'll be a father in less than a month."

"Give her my love. And tell A.J. I haven't forgotten that he owes me a chance to reclaim the family chess championship. I've been practicing. I won't be such easy pickings next time." He still couldn't believe that he, former president of his college chess club, had been roundly defeated by a ten-year-old kid.

Jon laughed. "I'm sure he'll be more than happy to trounce you again whenever you like."

Ben snorted, then explained the real reason he'd called. He told Jon where he was and what little he'd found out so far, then added, "I need you to do something for me, bro."

"Yeah, I thought you might. What is it?"

"I want you to check out a couple of people for priors. Confidence scams, most likely."

"Okay, I've got a pen. Let's have 'em."

"The first is a self-proclaimed psychic and fortune-teller. Rosalyn Carmody, or at least that's the name she's using now. She's in her fifties, I guess—silver hair, violet eyes."

"Got a hometown for her?"

"No, not yet. If I learn anything else, I'll let you know."

"Right. And the other name?"

"A magician. Milo the Magnificent. About the same age. They might have worked together before."

"You think they're working a scam on Andie McBride?"

"It's a possibility," Ben said. "She seems convinced Carmody's for real. I think she'd believe anything the woman tells her."

"Gullible type, is she?"

"Her family seems to think so," Ben replied, but he thought of the intelligence he'd seen gleaming in Andie's dark eyes and wondered if he was making a big mistake. "Even if she's not normally gullible, she certainly seems to have been taken in this time. She's even sharing a house with the psychic."

"Is there money involved?"

"Don't know yet. I wouldn't think she'd have a lot of money to risk, but her family is genuinely concerned, especially her grandmother. Apparently Andie wrote something in her letters to make her grandmother think there's something fishy going on with Andie's so-called psychic friend."

"Sounds like you agree."

"Maybe," Ben admitted. "You know how I feel about con artists. It's obvious this woman has convinced Andie she's a genuine psychic. Now I'm trying to find out if there's anything else she's trying to sell her. And I want to know how the magician is involved."

"Okay. I'll run these names, see what I can come up with. If you find out anything else about them, give me a call."

"Right." Ben gave his brother the number of his hotel. "Thanks, Jon. I owe you one."

"I remember owing you a few. Let's call it even."

Ben disconnected, knowing he hadn't given Jon much to work with. But at least it was a start. He wanted to find out what was going on here quickly so he could make a report to Andie's family and then get back to his own life. This wasn't the way he'd envisioned spending his first vacation in more than a year.

He glanced at his watch. It was still nearly four hours until the time he'd agreed to meet Andie. Since he had no intention of spending those hours cooped up in a boring hotel room, he decided to head to the park. He'd bought a season pass so he didn't have to pay the eighteen-buck admission every time he entered. He made a mental note to keep an accounting of his other expenses for Andie's family. Donald the stuffy dentist had promised to reimburse Ben for everything, and Ben had every intention of having him do so. He had better uses for his money than blowing it at a dumb theme park.

ANDIE REACHED into a pocket of her baggy overalls and pulled out a huge bouquet of paper flowers that sprouted as if by magic when she held them up. A chorus of admiring squeals rewarded her dramatic gesture. Mugging for all she was worth, she presented the flowers to a dark-eyed little girl in a wheelchair, whose delighted smile of appreciation warmed Andie all the way to her size-thirteen shoes.

Feeling rather proud of herself, she waved the small crowd of onlookers on and turned to move to another section of the park. She had to stop quickly before she ran into Ben Sherman's broad chest. This was becoming a habit—a rather pleasant one actually, she thought as her pulse leapt into high gear.

"Sorry." He motioned with one hand toward the wheelchair in which the little girl clutched her paper flowers. "That was very nicely done."

Extremely conscious of her ridiculous appearance, Andie linked her gloved hands in front of her. "She's a sweetheart."

"You must really like kids."

"Yes, very much," Andie said. "Why else would I be doing this?"

"Why, indeed?" he murmured, then took a bite of his half-eaten loaded hot dog.

"Lunch?" Andie asked with a smile.

He swallowed. "Late breakfast."

"How nutritious."

He shrugged. "It's hard to hang around here without overindulging in junk food."

"Tell me about it," she said. "I've gained ten pounds since I started working here."

His eyebrows lifted. "You must have been thin as a rail when you started, then. As far as I can tell, you haven't an ounce to spare now."

She felt herself blushing and was thankful now for her heavy makeup. It was ridiculous to react so dramatically to his offhand comment, she scolded herself sternly. "Are you gathering more material for your article this morning?"

"Mm. Any recommendations?"

Remembering Rosalyn's request, Andie motioned down the midway. "The fortune-teller's tent is about halfway down the midway. You mentioned you wanted to interview Rosalyn—she said you'd be welcome to talk to her. Maybe you'll even get your fortune read," she suggested with a forced smile.

Ben immediately looked scornful. "I think I'll pass on that part," he muttered. "But I would like to talk to her—for my article," he added.

"Ben," Andie said impulsively, catching his arm, "please be nice to her. She's such a sweet lady, and she has a lot of problems right now. Please don't make fun of what she does. What she is."

Ben looked from her gloved hand resting on his arm to her earnest painted face. "I won't make fun of her," he promised a bit gruffly. "Just don't ask me to pretend I believe any of her psychic mumbo jumbo, okay?"

Disappointed with his response, she dropped her hand and nodded stiffly. "I'd better get back to work. I have to pick up some balloons to pass out around the park."

"Fine. I'll see you at two, then."

"Yes," she agreed, wishing she had a good reason to decline. She told herself it was only the thought of Mr. Parker's certain disapproval that kept her quiet. That seemed much safer than admitting she wanted to see Ben Sherman again, no matter how uncomfortable he made her.

A child's squeal brought her attention back to her job. "Hi, clown! Can I shake your hand?"

Andie turned with a broad grin and an exaggerated start of surprise to mug for the two children approaching her so eagerly. So trustingly. For a fleeting moment, she wished she had their ability to accept things—and people—at face value. Maybe then she wouldn't be driving herself half-crazy wondering whether Ben Sherman was really the travel writer he claimed to be.

# 3

IT WAS A SLOW DAY at the park. Ben, having noticed the
sparse crowds when he'd arrived, had wondered if all
Sundays were this slow and if the park was struggling
to stay in business. The lines for even the most popular
rides weren't particularly long, and many of the midway game booths were sitting idle, their operators desperately trying to drum up business with their shouted
promises of potential prizes.

He paused when he spotted Milo the Magnificent
leaving the colorful fortune-teller's tent. Apparently
Milo and Rosalyn spent quite a bit of time together,
which made Ben all the more wary of their influence on
Andie, who seemed fond of them both.

A colorful placard, decorated with cosmic-looking
symbols, invited guests of the park to enter the tent and
be "amazed, bemused and delighted" with the fortune-
teller's talents. This attraction, it added in smaller print,
was included in the price of general admission to the
park. Feeling rather foolish, Ben impatiently pushed
aside several long strands of beads hanging in the en-
tranceway and entered the tent.

A bored-looking young woman in a yellow caftan
glanced up from behind a counter just inside. "Take a
number, please, and have a seat."

Though he lifted an expressive eyebrow at the rows of completely empty chairs behind her, Ben ripped a slip of paper from an automatic dispenser on the counter. There was no one else waiting, but if she wanted him to take a number, he'd take a number.

He didn't have to wait long. Less than ten minutes had passed before two elderly ladies came through a curtain on the far side of the waiting area, their gray heads close together as they talked rapidly and excitedly.

"She knew so many things about me. I could hardly believe it!" one was telling the other.

"Me, either. I thought I'd faint when she described my poor Edgar to a T."

"She said Edgar would want you to have someone new in your life. Haven't I been saying for ages that you should accept that nice Mr. Cunningham's invitations to dinner?"

"Yes, but how could she have known about Mr. Cunningham? I never even . . ."

Ben was still shaking his head in disgust after the ladies had vanished out onto the midway. He waited for his turn behind the curtain, feeling more like a fool than ever.

A soft chime sounded through the empty waiting area. The bored woman behind the counter glanced up from her paperback. "Number sixteen."

Ben glanced automatically down at the slip of paper in his hand. "Yeah," he muttered. "Sixteen."

"You can go in now."

He swallowed a sarcastic rejoinder and pushed through the heavy brocade curtain.

Rosalyn Carmody was sitting at a small round table in a tiny fabric-walled room. She was wearing something soft and floating again—deep emerald, this time—and the glittering bird pin. Three empty chairs were arranged around the table. She motioned him toward the one nearest her right side. "Mr. Sherman. How nice to see you again. Please join me."

"What?" he asked, glancing at the bare tabletop as he dropped into the chair. "No crystal ball? No tarot cards?"

"I have no need of props."

"Is that right?"

She only smiled and offered him one small lined hand. "May I have your right hand, please?"

"You read palms?" he asked as he reluctantly placed his hand in hers. It annoyed him that he immediately felt that tingly sensation again when they made contact.

How did she *do* that? Was she rubbing her feet against the carpet or something? Or was he more susceptible to suggestion than he'd believed?

"No, I don't read palms. But sometimes I pick up more about a person if we're touching as we talk," she explained, closing her fingers around his with surprising strength.

"I really didn't come in here to have my fortune told, you know," he said, trying to be polite. "I wanted to talk to you for my article—"

"Mr., um, Sherman, let's make a deal, shall we?" she interrupted him gently. "You don't have to pretend to believe in my abilities if I don't have to pretend to believe you're writing an article for a travel magazine."

He froze. "What do you mean?"

She frowned faintly, her eyes searching his face. "You're here because of Andie. I can sense that you mean her no harm, that you are concerned about her, so I must assume you are representing her family. She told me they were anxious about her and have been trying to determine her location ever since she left home four months ago. You're not a policeman . . . hmm. A private investigator?"

Hell. He'd been made. "What did you do, have someone toss my hotel room?" he asked gruffly, too disconcerted to remember to pull his hand from hers for the moment.

*This is what happens when you start getting cocky, Luck. You find yourself outsmarted by a dippy little old lady and an old magician who's obviously not as incompetent as he looks.*

Rosalyn seemed amused by his suggestion. "No, Ben, I didn't have anyone break into your hotel room. So, you admit I'm right?"

He could have bitten his tongue. "I'm not admitting anything, dammit."

Rosalyn was looking at his hand now, frowning in concentration. "You're very good at what you do. You work for yourself—you haven't the patience or the tact to answer to anyone else. You're very close to your family—I see siblings. You're the youngest—"

Ben opened his mouth to set her straight.

"No," she said decisively before he could speak. "Not the youngest. The middle child."

"Look, this is—"

"Someone hurt you once. A woman."

He jerked as though she'd bitten him. He tried to snatch his hand away, found that he couldn't, and stared in confusion at the tiny hand holding his so firmly. How could someone so small and fragile have a grip like that?

"You mustn't blame yourself for a youthful error in judgment, Ben," Rosalyn advised him kindly. "Everyone makes mistakes. You really shouldn't continue to avoid commitments just because one woman wasn't worthy of your love. You have a great deal to offer some fortunate woman. I see a long happy marriage in store for you—once you stop fighting your fears and learn to trust again."

This time she didn't try to stop him when he pulled his hand away. He clenched his fists on his knees beneath the table and glared at her. "You're good, lady, I can say that. I don't know if you're an expert at running fast background checks or just a hell of a lucky guesser, but—"

"I've made you nervous. I'm sorry."

"I'm *not* nervous," Ben all but shouted back at her, rankled by her choice of words. "If you'd just be quiet a minute and let me —"

"Dammit, Ben, you promised you'd be nice to her. Stop yelling at her!" Andie's voice interrupted loudly from behind him.

Ben whirled in his chair and stared at the thoroughly angry clown glaring at him from an inconspicuous doorway at the back of the tent. Her gloved hands were fisted on her slender hips and her dark eyes were snapping fire within her painted face. One oversize shoe tapped furiously against the floor.

Her broad painted-on smile looked wildly incongruous beneath her fierce scowl. Had Ben not been so disgusted with himself for blowing his cover—and this assignment—he might have found the sight amusing. "You were eavesdropping?" he demanded.

"No. I just got here," she snapped back. "Just in time to hear you yelling at Rosalyn. And you promised you'd only ask her a few questions for your article."

He looked at Rosalyn, waiting for her to fill Andie in on his true identity. The woman looked amused as she turned to her enraged champion. "Now, Andie, dear, you know some people aren't comfortable with telepathy. Mr. Sherman is one of those people who finds it difficult to accept that which can't be easily explained. I'm afraid I disconcerted him by telling him a few things he wasn't quite prepared to hear."

What the hell? Rosalyn wasn't blowing his cover? Ben narrowed his eyes as a sudden explanation occurred to him. She was probably going to offer him a bribe. She'd keep quiet about who he really was in exchange for . . . what? Money? His own silence?

"Was there something in particular you wanted, Andie, or were you just checking to make sure Mr. Sherman was being nice to me?" Rosalyn asked with a smile.

Andie gave Ben one last scowl, then turned to the older woman. "Milo asked me to tell you he can't join you for lunch, after all. He broke one of his props this morning and has to get it repaired before the performance tomorrow."

"Thank you, dear. Perhaps I'll take a sandwich to him later. I'm sure he'll forget to eat until his precious equipment is repaired."

"You're probably right." Andie nodded, then turned to Ben. "I was just going over to the petting-zoo area. Maybe you'd like to join me?" she asked, obviously hoping to get him away from her friend.

"Not now, thanks. Rosalyn was just telling me I'd be meeting someone tall, dark and gorgeous," he lied evenly. "I think I'll hang around a few minutes and get more details."

Andie hesitated, reluctant to leave them alone. Rosalyn laughed lightly and waved her on. "Go ahead, dear. The children in the park are waiting for you. Mr. Sherman will find you later."

The look Andie gave Ben was hardly that of a jolly clown. In fact, it promised all sorts of dire consequences if he started yelling at her friend again.

He waited until she was gone before spinning back to face the fortune-teller. "All right, why didn't you tell her?"

"About why you're here? Oh, I think you'll tell her that yourself. When you're ready."

Ben waited a minute then when she didn't say anything else, asked, "That's it? You're willing to keep this secret from your 'friend'?"

"Andie *is* my friend, Ben. A very dear friend," Rosalyn replied in a voice that somehow combined steel with velvet. "I wouldn't allow anyone to hurt her if I could help it. Fortunately I'm convinced that your intentions toward her are entirely harmless, though I don't approve of your methods. Deceptions are so hard to maintain, you understand. I don't think this one was your idea, though. Her family's suggestion?"

Ben remained stubbornly silent, waiting for the subtle offer he was sure would follow.

Rosalyn smiled and patted his arm, almost fondly. "You'll be good for Andie," she murmured. "Strong, dependable, loyal and protective. Yet you'll know when to give her the freedom she has craved for so long, and the independence she was never granted by her family. I'm glad you're here, Benjamin."

One of them was crazy. Ben wondered rather dazedly if it was him. "That's it? You're not going to offer me any deals? Ask for an exchange of favors?"

Rosalyn was unperturbed. "Why would I want to offer you a deal? It seems to me you're the one with something to hide. Andie knows all *my* secrets."

*I'll bet*, he thought with a snort of disbelief. But there wasn't really anything else he could say for the moment. As Rosalyn had so skillfully pointed out, she had the upper hand. For now. She could probably prove he wasn't who he'd claimed to be, while all he had was a barrelful of suspicions.

He'd have to see what he could do about that. But first it looked as though he was going to have to tell Andie who he really was, and why he was here. Before someone else took care of that little chore for him and blew any chance he might have of smoothing things over with her.

A bell rang quietly somewhere above them, and Rosalyn glanced toward the brocade curtain. "I'm afraid your time is up, Ben. I have others waiting to talk to me. I'm sure we'll be seeing quite a bit more of each other."

"You can count on that," he promised, shoving himself to his feet.

Rosalyn only smiled and looked thoroughly at ease as he quickly left the tiny room.

ANDIE WAS STILL fuming when she stepped out of her dressing room that afternoon, face scrubbed clean and clown costume exchanged for a colorful knit shorts-and-top set. Every time she thought of the way Ben had talked to Rosalyn her blood boiled. She didn't care what Rosalyn said; she could see no excuse for Ben to have reacted so fiercely. If he thought she was going to meekly cooperate with his interview now, he had another think coming!

"Hey, Andie," a male voice drawled from behind her. She glanced over her shoulder. A slender blond man leaned against a wall of the hallway, deftly juggling four balls. His felt fedora, pale yellow long-sleeved shirt, striped suspenders and baggy pleated slacks could have come straight from the wardrobe room of *Guys and Dolls.*

"Hi, Blake. Were you waiting for me?"

Blake had asked Andie out a couple of times when he'd first started working at the park about a month ago. He was a wickedly attractive, smoothly charming fellow, and she'd been flattered that he'd noticed her, but she'd always found some excuse to decline. Maybe because Blake was a bit *too* smooth.

"No." Blake shifted into a new pattern, bouncing each ball off the grubby floor before catching it and sending it arcing above his head with the others. "Just hanging out."

"Oh. Well, see you later, then."

"I hear you're being interviewed for a travel magazine."

"Yes," she corroborated reluctantly.

"Parker's been telling everyone about it. He's tickled pink that the park is finally getting some promotion. You'll probably get a raise if business picks up because of it."

*And probably get fired if I fail to cooperate now,* Andie reminded herself. She had a lot to lose if she told Ben Sherman exactly what she thought of him. "I haven't been offered a raise, but I wouldn't turn one down," she quipped. "Now, if you'll excuse me, I'm supposed to meet someone."

Blake switched rhythm again, tossing the balls up two at a time, so it appeared that two were always in the air and two in his hands. "About this writer . . ."

Andie shifted her weight, wishing Blake would get to the point, knowing he'd do so in his own good time— as this enigmatic man seemed to do everything. "What about him?"

The colorful balls leapt and arced, dancing in front of him as if they had a life of their own. Blake appeared to give them his full attention, though Andie was aware that his actions were almost automatic. "Milo's worried about him. Said he's not sure the guy's exactly what he says he is. I gather he got that impression from Rosalyn."

Andie bit her lower lip, remembering Rosalyn's gentle warning. *Don't take everything at face value.* "Why wouldn't Rosalyn tell me if she suspects Ben's hiding something?"

Blake managed to shrug without interrupting the movement of the balls. "Just thought I'd mention it. Nice girls like you tend to be too trusting of people," he added with a mocking, but not unkind, smile. "People like me, on the other hand, instinctively look for the worst in everyone. And we usually find it."

It annoyed Andie greatly that even self-absorbed Blake seemed to think he had to protect her. Why was it that no one ever believed she was fully capable of taking care of herself? Not her family, not her friends— not even casual acquaintances like Blake apparently.

"I appreciate your concern," she lied with an attempt at graciousness, "but I can't see that there's any harm in my answering a few questions about the park for this man. After all, Mr. Parker is the one who asked me to cooperate. I'm only doing my job."

Blake caught the balls and stuffed them in the oversize pockets of his baggy slacks. His bright blue eyes met hers with an intensity that held her captive for a moment. "Just watch your step, okay? And if the guy does anything or asks anything that makes you uncomfortable, let somebody know. Rosalyn, or Milo, or me. Will you do that?"

"I think you're all overreacting," she said with some asperity. "But if it makes you feel better, I'll let someone know if he does anything weird."

"Good. See you around, Andie."

Andie watched him disappear down the long hallway, then shook her head in exasperation. Honestly, circus people were so obsessed with privacy, she thought, turning toward the exit. The unspoken rule to accept the present and ignore the past had been made clear to her from the beginning; they didn't ask questions, didn't swap histories, rarely even swapped surnames.

She'd wanted to make sweeping changes when she'd left her dull routines in Seattle, and she could certainly say that everything was very different from what she'd been accustomed to. She'd met some very unusual people—some of them nice, some not so nice, but none of them boring. And no matter where her path took her next, she'd never regret the decision she'd made several months earlier to break away from her old life and embark on a new one.

Now, if only she could convince everyone she'd made changes within herself, as well. That she no longer needed to be guided and protected like a naive sheltered innocent.

IT WAS A QUARTER after two when Andie finally stepped outside and found Ben Sherman waiting for her. He was leaning against the trunk of a tree, one foot propped behind him, his head tipped back as he drained the remains of a canned soft drink. He looked lean and fit and strong in his striped knit shirt and denim shorts, well-defined muscles bulging in his bare arms and legs. He didn't look like a writer, a man who spent much time sitting behind a typewriter or computer, she found herself thinking.

And then she shook her head in self-disgust. Now she was letting everyone else's paranoia get to her. After all, Mr. Parker had approved him and his reason for being here, so Ben must have had some proof of his identity and probably samples of his work.

Rosalyn had hinted that Ben wasn't quite what he appeared, but she hadn't seemed worried about him. If Rosalyn sensed some reason to be concerned about Ben, she'd have said so. Especially since Rosalyn, of all people, had every reason to be wary of strangers. The psychic's very life depended on her intuition, Andie thought with a shiver of unease.

"Judging by that fierce expression, I take it you're still mad at me," Ben drawled as he tossed his soft-drink can into a trash receptacle and stepped away from the tree.

She formed a mental picture of a frowning Mr. Parker before she answered with a measure of civility, "I'll continue to help you with your article as long as you promise to treat my housemate with the courtesy she deserves."

"All right. That's a promise."

There was something about his tone she didn't quite trust. Andie searched his gleaming green eyes for a long moment, then conceded with a slight sigh, "All right. You said you wanted a behind-the-scenes tour of the park this afternoon. Where would you like to begin?"

He made an expansive gesture with one arm. "You're the guide. I'll put myself entirely in your hands."

This time she *knew* she shouldn't trust his too-innocent tone. Instead, she ignored it.

"We'll start with the animal barns," she said abruptly, turning away from him. *And I truly hope you step in something that matches your attitude*, she thought sardonically.

# 4

BEN HAD BEEN PREPARED to level with Andie about his identity as soon as he saw her. He hadn't wanted this deception in the first place, and he hated the thought of the psychic and the magician having anything to hold over his head. Her family surely wouldn't expect him to carry on even after his cover was blown to the others. He was cursing himself for that carelessness when Andie emerged from the dressing room, utterly beautiful in her colorful knit shorts set, sunlight glinting in her long dark hair and suspicion mirrored in her sultry brown eyes.

He decided that he'd find the right time to tell her everything—later.

Though she was a bit cool toward him at first, Andie was totally cooperative in showing him around the park. If he *had* been writing a travel article, she would have made an excellent source. In less than two hours, she'd shown him everything there was to see of the three-year-old theme park, fully answering his questions about the park's operations, even anticipating other questions before he thought to ask them. Just for appearances, he took a few notes in the pocket-size notebook he usually carried, but many of the questions he asked were prompted by genuine curiosity as much as for the sake of his precarious cover.

"Is the park open year round?" he asked.

Andie shook her head. "The first of April through the end of October," she explained. "It's closed during the winter months."

"Where do all the employees go during the off-season?"

"A skeleton crew stays on to take care of the grounds and the animals. Many of the summer staff are high-school or college students who go back to school in the fall. Some of the employees travel with carnivals in the warmer climates, I understand. I don't know about the others."

Ben really didn't care what the others would do during the off-season. "What will *you* do?"

She shrugged. "I don't know yet. Find a temporary job somewhere, I suppose. Maybe sign up as a temp with an agency in Dallas. I'm flexible," she added. Her smile showed her contentment with that life-style.

Ben wasn't satisfied, but he let it go and turned his attention back to the park.

The park employees seemed to be typical of the carnivals and circuses Ben had frequented in his youth. Some of them were tough-looking, others young and eager, most rather eccentric. Cigarettes and tattoos seemed to be popular among both male and female carnies.

He gestured down the colorful main midway and asked, "Are those games really on the up-and-up, or are they rigged to the park's advantage? I see a lot of small prizes being carried around, but not many of those big stuffed animals that are so enticingly displayed above the booths."

Andie lifted her chin defensively. "I can assure you that every game here at Big Top is perfectly legitimate. Even if Mr. Parker wanted to run a crooked operation, which he does not, the local authorities wouldn't permit it. Obviously the games are constructed to be quite challenging, but they aren't rigged to be impossible to win."

"Don't get mad again. It was a fair question," Ben said reasonably. "Everyone's heard of games with switches or other hidden mechanical devices that let the operators choose who wins and who loses."

"Not here," she insisted stubbornly. "In fact, I think you should try a few of them. On the house."

"That's really not—"

"I insist," she said, and the glint in her eye told him she'd issued a challenge that he'd darned well better be prepared to accept.

He sighed. "All right, I'll try a few of them. But I'm paying to play, just like everyone else."

"Fine. Shall we start with this one?" she asked, motioning toward a row of painted milk cans behind a bunting-draped counter.

Inside the booth, a thin young man with long stringy hair tried to entice passersby to take a chance at winning one of the enormous purple dinosaurs hanging over his head. "Win a prize for your little girl," he shouted at one passing father. "One softball in a can gets you a small prize, two in and you win one of these big beauties. Come on, give it a try. You know she wants a dinosaur."

"Please, Daddy," the carrot-topped little girl said eagerly, boucing at her father's feet. "You can do that. It looks easy."

The auburn-haired man, who looked to Ben like an unathletic type, nervously eyed the marginally larger-than-softball-size opening in the cans. "I don't know, Laurie. I've never been much of a pitcher."

"Let me show you how it's done," the young hawker said, leaping agilely over the counter. He picked up two softballs and tossed them toward the cans, one after the other. Both went in.

"See?" he said, turning back toward the father. "Piece of cake."

The little girl bounced harder. "You can do it, Daddy. Try it, okay?"

"Well, maybe just once," the man conceded, taking a reluctant step toward the booth.

"Two balls for a dollar," the game operator said promptly, as he returned to his place behind the counter.

Ben knew the man wasn't going to win anything as soon as he picked up a ball. The guy looked as though he'd never held a softball in his life. Sure enough, neither ball went in—not even close.

"Try again," the hawker urged, tossing a softball from one hand to another. "You just need a little practice. Come on, pal, it's only another buck."

The man looked rather desperately from the milk cans to the little girl at his side, who was longingly eyeing the huge purple dinosaurs hanging just out of reach. "Just try one more time, Daddy," she said. "That's all. I promise."

Ben glanced at Andie, who looked decidedly uncomfortable and avoided his eyes. Then he turned back to watch as the beleaguered father shelled out another dollar and, with a look of grim determination, picked up two softballs.

He got closer that time. One of the balls actually hit the rim of a milk can and circled it a time or two before dropping—to the outside of the can. Looking embarrassed, the man patted his daughter's head. "Sorry, pumpkin," he murmured. "You know I'm more familiar with computers than baseballs. Come on, I'll buy you an ice-cream cone."

"Okay, Daddy." She gave him a smile that assured him she loved him even if he couldn't hit the side of a barn.

"Let me try that," Ben said impulsively, stepping up to the counter with a dollar in hand.

The young man behind the counter looked around eagerly, then spotted Andie. "Oh, hi, Andie. Friend of yours?"

She hesitated only a moment before answering. "Yes. Tommy, this is Ben. He wants to try a few of the games."

"Sure. No problem. Two balls for a buck."

Ben had already laid his dollar on the counter. He eyed the milk cans, estimating the slight angle at which they were sitting. As Andie had explained, the games were designed to give an advantage to the park, but he couldn't see anything to indicate the game was unfairly rigged.

The father and daughter had started to walk away, but the man paused when Ben stepped up to the counter. "Wait a minute, honey. I want to see this," he murmured to the girl.

Ben had been barely old enough to stand on his own when he and his brother had played their first game of catch. He'd been playing for his own entertainment ever since. It annoyed him greatly that he overcompensated for the milk can's angle on his first pitch; the ball hit the edge of the hole, bounced out and landed on the ground beside the can. He could almost hear his brother's hoot of derision.

"See, Daddy. *He* can't do it, either," the little girl whispered loudly.

Setting his jaw, Ben tightened his grip on the second ball, took careful aim and released it in a gentle arc. The ball plopped easily into a milk can.

"A winner!" the game operator announced loudly, tossing Ben a small teddy bear. "Want to try again? You can trade three small prizes for one big dinosaur."

Ben set down another dollar. "Yeah," he muttered, handing Andie the teddy bear. "Let me try again."

"Uh . . . Ben," Andie murmured.

He ignored her.

This time both balls went into the milk cans. Ben nodded in grim satisfaction as the hawker called everyone's attention to the win. The production he made of taking down a purple dinosaur and depositing it into Ben's arms drew a small crowd of interested onlookers.

Ben turned to the little girl and her father. With a lifted eyebrow, he silently asked permission to give the toy to the child. The father nodded with a rueful smile. "Played a bit of ball, have you?" he asked, one hand on his daughter's shoulder.

"Pitched for my college baseball team," Ben explained. He handed the toy to the little girl. "Your dad would have gotten it next time," he said in a low voice. "He was pretty close with that last throw."

The child's eyes brightened as her arms closed around the garish stuffed animal. "Is it okay, Daddy?" she asked, looking up for his approval.

"Sure, honey," her father answered, ruffling her bright hair. "Tell the man thank-you."

"Thank you," she said obediently, hugging the purple dinosaur enthusiastically.

"You're welcome," Ben answered with a smile.

A woman pushing a baby in a stroller joined the father and daughter as they were leaving the booth. "Elliot!" Ben heard her exclaim. "*You* won a prize pitching softballs?"

"No. Someone else did," the father explained. "But I was beginning to figure out the angles . . ."

Their voices faded as they disappeared into the milling crowds. Ben chuckled and turned back to Andie, who was still holding the little teddy bear. She looked at him with lifted eyebrows. "I take it you don't like to lose."

Ben cleared his throat self-consciously. "No," he admitted. "I don't like to lose."

He wondered if he only imagined that her expression suddenly grew more wary. "Shall we continue our tour?" she asked politely, taking a step away from him.

"Sure. Why not."

They didn't stop at any of the other game booths. Ben assured Andie he was convinced the park was operated in a manner that was as legitimate as any legal carnival. She didn't look particularly pleased by the backhanded compliment, but didn't challenge him on it. Instead, she took him to one of the sideshows in which eager college-age kids did an enthusiastic song-and-dance routine entitled "Back to the Fifties."

Born in the early sixties himself, Ben didn't bother to point out the irony of nineties teens in poodle skirts and ponytails singing songs that had been recorded long before they'd been born. Instead, he sat back and enjoyed the show—and the feel of having Andie sitting close at his side.

"What would you like to see next?" Andie asked when the musical review ended.

"Food," Ben answered promptly as the tantalizing scent of grilled Polish sausages, peppers and onions wafted past his nose.

Andie laughed. "I should have known."

Shadows were lengthening over the midway when Ben finally declared himself sated after downing a nutritionist's nightmare meal of sausage, peppers and onions on a bun dripping with mustard, a side order of fried potatoes and a pineapple sundae for dessert. Andie had chosen a grilled chicken sandwich followed by a scoop of frozen yogurt.

"We've seen all of the park operations except the rides," Ben commented, his attention captured by the neon lights just flickering to life around him. The sounds of rock music, calliope tunes, laughter, squeals, shouting game operators and mothers calling out to their children blended into a loud cheerful background.

A bass-heavy beat drew him forward to the Himalaya, a ride in which connected two-seater cars spun at dizzying speeds around a steeply graded track to the accompaniment of deafening rock and roll music. An overly amplified disc jockey encouraged riders to scream their pleasure. "Want to ride that with me?" Ben asked Andie.

She shook her head. "Anything that spins around makes me horribly ill," she admitted. "Especially this soon after eating."

"I guess the Rocket is out, then," he said regretfully, looking up at a vertical ride that spun its riders head over heels in round metal baskets.

"For me it is," she said firmly. "But go ahead and ride if you like. I'll watch."

"Nah. Wouldn't be any fun alone." He glanced to his right and brightened. "Here we go. The Ferris wheel. No one gets sick on the Ferris wheel."

"People who are terrified of heights do," she retorted.

"Oh." He turned back to face her. "Are you terrified of heights?"

"No."

He grinned. "Then you'll ride with me?"

"Sure. Everyone should see the park from the top of the Ferris wheel. Especially in the evening, when all the lights are on."

"Sounds very romantic," Ben said, lowering his voice to an intimate level.

Andie ignored him. "The line forms over here," she said, and walked away. He followed eagerly.

Riding the towering Ferris wheel on a summer evening, with the multicolored lights of the park spread beneath them and the cheerful sounds muted by distance, was very romantic indeed. The tiny car in which they rode forced them to sit close together, shoulders and thighs touching. Ben's bare leg pressed against Andie's, and he was glad they'd both worn shorts.

The wheel made a swooping, gravity-defying descent, then started back up. Ben and Andie exchanged a laughing glance as two teenage girls in the gondola beneath them squealed loudly. The ride came to a halt when Ben and Andie were perched right at the top, leaving them to swing gently there as new riders climbed on at the bottom.

"It's beautiful up here, isn't it?" Andie asked.

"Mm." But Ben's eyes weren't on the glittering panorama spread below. Instead, he looked at Andie, admiring the way reflections of the colored light bulbs around them danced in her dark eyes and made her flawless skin glow intriguingly. "Beautiful," he murmured.

She glanced his way, then froze at the look on his face. "Um, Ben..." she began.

He leaned over and kissed her without giving her warning of his intentions. The kiss was brief, but thorough. Ben enjoyed it every bit as much as he'd expected to. It took a great effort for him to draw back, when what he really wanted to do was to keep kissing her.

Andie's eyes were huge when he pulled away. "Ben?"

"Tradition," he said lightly, touching a fingertip to the tip of her nose. "Every guy knows the top of the Ferris wheel is a perfect place to snatch a kiss."

She cleared her throat and made a visible effort to match his casual tone. "Is that right?"

"Yeah. Want to ride the spook train with me next?"

"So I'll get scared and grab you, right?"

He grinned. "Right. That's the second trick every guy learns about amusement-park rides."

The Ferris wheel started to move again with a slight lurch that made Andie's fingers tighten on the safety bar. "Since I'm aware of your scheme, I don't think there's any reason for us to ride the spook train," she said.

"Oh." He exaggerated his disappointment. "Well, feel free to hold on to me, anyway."

She smiled and looked away. When they returned to ground level and the ride attendant released their safety bar she leapt out of the snug gondola. Ben hoped her rather flustered behavior meant that the brief kiss had affected her as much as it had him.

The moment they stepped away from the Ferris wheel, Andie began to lead the way rapidly toward the park exit. Looked like the tour was over, Ben thought ruefully. What excuse could he use now to keep her with him a bit longer?

Andie came to such a sudden stop that Ben, hurrying behind, almost ran into her. He put his hands on her shoulders to steady himself, and instantly felt the tension thrumming through her. "What's wrong?" he asked.

She was staring down the midway. "Something's going on at the fortune-teller's tent."

He followed her gaze. Sure enough, a small crowd had gathered outside the tent. As they watched, someone dressed in a park medic's uniform pushed through the spectators and ducked inside.

"Oh, my God," Andie whispered, her voice strained. "He's found her!"

With that, she broke away from Ben and ran toward the tent. Ben followed, his head spinning with questions. What was happening? Who was "he" and who had he found?

*What the hell was going on here?*

HER HEART POUNDING, Andie pushed through the chattering crowd standing between her and the opening of the fortune-teller's tent. A rather unkempt man with a scantily dressed bleached blonde clinging to his tattooed bicep solidly blocked her path. "Please," she murmured, her voice strained. "Please let me through."

With a disgruntled mumble, the man moved, and Andie slipped past him. She was aware that Ben followed close behind, but her mind was on the terrifying possibilities that she might find inside Rosalyn's tent.

Someone stepped in front of her just as she reached the doorway. "Sorry," a man's voice said, "no one can go in ri— Oh, it's you, Andie."

Andie clutched the long sleeve of Blake's pale blue shirt. "Blake, what's wrong? What's happened?"

"Rosalyn collapsed," he answered, his handsome face unusually grim beneath the brim of his fedora.

Andie realized this was one of the few times she'd seen Blake without his typical lazy smile. He looked different without it—rather dangerous actually. She quickly released his shirt. "Is she all right? Can I go in?"

He moved out of her way. "Yeah, go on in. I think she's okay, but they're checking her out now."

Andie started past him. Blake moved behind her, intercepting Ben, who started to protest the interference. "It's okay, Blake," Andie said automatically. "He's with me."

Again Blake moved and Ben followed Andie inside.

Rosalyn was sitting in the little chair behind her table, her face pale, her silvery hair disheveled. Several people hovered around her: Pam, the young ticket taker, looking distraught; two park medics in crisp blue shirts with plastic ID badges clipped to the pockets; and Milo, who held Rosalyn's hand and patted it as though to reassure himself she was all right.

"Rosalyn?" Andie took her housemate's free hand and knelt at her side. "Are you all right? What happened?"

"Andie, what are you still doing at the park?" Rosalyn asked, her voice reassuringly strong.

"I've been showing Ben around."

Rosalyn glanced past her to Ben. "Oh. Hello, Ben. Did you have a nice afternoon?"

"Rosalyn!" Andie interrupted, frustrated. "Blake said you collapsed."

Embarrassed, Rosalyn shook her head. "It wasn't all that dramatic, I assure you. It was just one of my spells." She looked wryly at the medics. "You two can go back to your station now. I promise you I'm fine. Go take care of someone who really needs you."

"She refuses to go to a hospital for a full examination," one of the medics told Andie with a resigned look. "There's really nothing else we can do here."

"I'll talk to her," Andie promised. She turned back to the older woman as the medics left, followed by Pam. "Rosalyn—"

"Now, Andie, there's no reason to start nagging me about a hospital. I absolutely refuse to go. There's no need."

"So stubborn," Milo muttered, patting Rosalyn's hand more briskly. "Won't listen to anyone."

"Rosalyn, if you don't tell me what happened, I'm going to scream," Andie warned. "I really am."

Rosalyn made a clucking sound and shook her head. "I feel so foolish. I was counseling a very nice woman—"

"What are you doing still working?" Andie broke in with a sudden frown. "Your shift should have ended hours ago. You never work the night shift on Sundays."

"Jordanna wasn't feeling well again. She called in with a headache, and I said I'd take her shift today in exchange for some time off later this week. I didn't mind."

Andie shook her head in disapproval, but urged, "You were with a woman and . . . ?"

"She'd lost her grandmother's pearls," Rosalyn explained. "She was quite distressed about it, since the pearls had great sentimental value to her. I 'saw' them behind a heavy piece of furniture—a dresser perhaps. Oh, dear, I'm not sure I ever had the chance to tell her. Would someone look outside and see if she's still around? She has red hair and a bright purple—"

"Rosalyn! *What happened?*"

Rosalyn blinked. "Honestly, Andie, there's no need to shout."

Andie drew a deep breath and made a deliberate effort to speak more calmly. "I'm sorry. What happened next?"

Rosalyn glanced from Milo to Ben and then back to Andie. "I had a feeling . . . a very bad feeling. I suddenly found myself unable to breathe. I believe I must have blacked out for a moment. When I came to, the woman was shouting for help and Pam rushed in, and then someone called for Milo and the medics. I tried to tell everyone I was all right, but I was still feeling a bit woozy and having trouble expressing myself clearly."

Andie swallowed hard. "What sort of feeling did you have, Rosalyn? Did it have anything to do with—?" She broke off, aware of intently listening ears. Oh, why had she brought Ben in with her?

Rosalyn understood. "Possibly," she murmured. "I couldn't tell. I suddenly felt as though he . . . was close. Very close."

"Oh, my God," Andie whispered, her fingers tightening around Rosalyn's fragile hand. "Are you sure?"

"No. And the feeling's gone now. I'm not sensing anything. Perhaps I was just tired. I suppose I did rather overdo it today, working a double shift."

"You certainly did," Andie said briskly, rising to her feet. "I insist you go home this very minute and get some rest. The fortune-teller's tent can just be closed for the rest of the evening."

"I don't understand," Milo said suddenly, looking thoroughly bewildered. "*Who* did you sense was close? Rosalyn, my dear, are you in some sort of trouble? Is there anything I can do to help?"

Rosalyn's violet eyes softened as she looked at the paunchy magician. "No, Milo. As I told Andie, I'm sure

I'm just a bit tired. I suppose I'm getting too old for such long hours."

Milo's fond smile was so expressive that Andie's throat tightened. "Nonsense. You'll never be old, Rosalyn."

Rosalyn laughed softly. "How sweet."

Andie tugged gently at her housemate's hand. "Come on, Rosalyn. I'm taking you home. Are you sure you won't let me stop on the way and—"

"No hospitals," Rosalyn said firmly.

Andie sighed and surrendered, knowing that no amount of argument would sway Rosalyn.

She turned to find Ben watching her searchingly. "What's going on?" he asked in a low voice.

She shook her head. "She's just tired. I'm taking her home to rest now."

He didn't look at all satisfied by the explanation. "I'll follow you to make sure you both get home all right."

"Thank you, but that won't be necessary. I'm quite capable of taking care of this."

"I'm sure you are, but—"

"Rosalyn and I will be fine, Ben. Perhaps we'll see you again, or do you have enough material for your article now?" The possibility that this was goodbye gave her a hollow feeling deep inside.

"You'll see me again," he assured her, his expression making it a promise.

The hollow feeling changed to one of nervous anticipation. She tried not to think about that, as she took

Rosalyn's arm and led her toward the back exit of the tent, away from the curious crowd standing at the front.

BEN WATCHED GRIMLY as Andie escorted the older woman out with touching concern. Something strange was definitely going on here. Despite her bluffing, Rosalyn had looked genuinely frightened, and so had Andie. What had that crazy psychic gotten Andie involved in? And how was Ben going to make Andie trust him enough to tell him about it, especially once she discovered he'd been lying to her from the beginning?

Exhaling impatiently, he turned to Milo and noted that the older man looked a bit worn. "You okay?" he asked.

The magician nodded. "Too much excitement, I suppose. I believe I'll turn in early myself."

"You need a ride somewhere?" Ben felt compelled to offer.

Milo smiled and shook his head. "Thank you, but no. I live here at the park. I have one of the mobile homes parked in the back lot."

Ben nodded. "All right. I'll be seeing you around, Milo."

"Yes," Milo said slowly. "I expect you will."

Ben frowned, wondering what the older man had meant, but Milo had already turned and was walking toward the back exit.

Shaking his head at the strange conclusion to an unsettling day, Ben moved toward the front of the tent. For some reason, he had a sudden urge to get another look at the guy who'd tried to stop Andie and him from entering the fortune-teller's tent earlier. Andie had called him Blake, and Ben hadn't liked the way Blake had looked at her. Just how well did Andie know that guy, anyway?

But Blake, whoever he was, was gone when Ben walked outside. Pam was hanging a Closed sign over the door of the tent, explaining to the curious crowd that the fortune-teller wasn't feeling well and wouldn't be available for the remainder of the evening. A middle-aged woman with dyed red hair and a bright purple blouse moved in front of Ben as he walked out of the tent. "Excuse me, but is she all right? I was with her when she fainted. It frightened me half to death, I can tell you!" she said in a twangy Texas accent.

Ben nodded. "She's fine. Just overtired."

"Thank heavens."

Ben started to move past her, then stopped. "You the one who lost your grandmother's pearls?"

The woman's eyes widened behind trendy plastic-framed glasses. "Why, yes, I am."

"Look behind a heavy piece of furniture. A dresser maybe."

The woman gasped and covered her open mouth with one hand. "I'll do that! Thank you!"

Ben shrugged and kept walking, wondering why he'd passed along the psychic's message. It wasn't as though he believed it, but it seemed a logical place to look if a piece of jewelry was misplaced. Chances were, the woman would look behind her dresser, find the necklace and firmly believe for the rest of her life that supernatural forces had directed her to it. Some people were just too gullible, he thought with a disdainful shake of his head.

Just to make sure Andie and Rosalyn had reached home safely, Ben drove past their little house before returning to his hotel. Andie's car was parked in the driveway and lights glowed from the windows. Ben parked for a few minutes at the curb and carefully studied the house. Everything looked snug and secure, and the street was reassuringly quiet.

As he drove away, he wished he could shake the uneasy feeling that something threatening hovered just out of sight. He gave a snort of self-disgust.

He was letting this assignment get to him, he thought wryly. Psychics and magicians, colored lights and fancy facades. How was a guy supposed to know what was real amid all the illusion?

The only real moment in the strange day had been that kiss he'd shared with Andie at the top of the Ferris wheel. And that had been just a bit too real for comfort.

He knew he'd still be thinking about that kiss long into the night in his lonely room. And again he asked himself why the hell he'd allowed himself to be talked into this crazy mission.

# 5

ANDIE PACED the tiny living room of her rented house, pausing occasionally to peek out the window at the deserted nighttime street. She saw nothing to concern her, but that didn't particularly reassure her. It was what she *couldn't* see that scared her.

"Andie, please sit down and try to relax. You're making me nervous with all that pacing."

Andie turned back to Rosalyn with a grimace of apology. "I'm sorry. I guess I'm still keyed up from the scare you gave me earlier."

"Really, dear, you mustn't worry so much about me. I'm perfectly capable of taking care of myself."

"I wish I could believe that," Andie replied, nevertheless coming to sit beside Rosalyn on the worn sofa. "But we both know your special gifts aren't always reliable when it comes to your own circumstances. You told me your vision is much clearer with others than with yourself."

Rosalyn shook her head. "Sometimes I talk too much."

"Or not enough. Are you sure you've told me everything about what happened earlier?"

"Yes. Everything." There could be no doubting the sincerity of Rosalyn's response. "It was only a strange feeling, and it went away quickly. I'm almost convinced it was simply a result of working too many hours today. And I did skip lunch. Perhaps my blood sugar got too low or something like that."

"You shouldn't skip meals, Rosalyn. Your work is so draining for you. You need the energy."

Rosalyn chuckled.

Andie moaned and covered her face. "I'm doing it again, aren't I? I simply can't seem to get out of the habit of taking care of everyone around me."

"Everyone but yourself."

Andie dropped her hands. "That's over. I'm now fully responsible for my own welfare—totally independent for the first time in my life. And I love it."

"Mm."

"I do," Andie insisted, hearing skepticism. "I wouldn't go back to the life I was living before for anything."

"No," Rosalyn agreed. "Not to that life. But you won't be alone, either."

Andie frowned a bit at her housemate's tone; it was the one Rosalyn always used when she was making one of her uncanny predictions. "I'm not alone now," she said. "I have you and my other friends at the park."

Rosalyn smiled sweetly. "You need more than that. And you'll have it."

"Rosalyn . . ." Andie began uneasily.

Rosalyn only laughed and changed the subject. "Did you have a nice day with Benjamin?"

At least Andie *hoped* Rosalyn was changing the subject. The possibility that Ben was somehow involved with Rosalyn's mysterious hints made her very uncomfortable. "It was a nice day," she conceded carefully. "He asked a lot of questions about the park and I answered them. We saw a few shows, played one of the games and rode the Ferris wheel. And he ate. I've never seen anyone who can eat like that man." She gave an amused shake of her head. "It's a wonder he stays so trim."

"He does have quite a nice build, doesn't he? Strong chest, broad shoulders, tight little—"

"Rosalyn!"

Again Rosalyn's laughter pealed musically through the room. "I may be getting old, Andie, but there's nothing wrong with my eyesight."

"You're not old."

Rosalyn shook her head and stood. "Sometimes I feel it. I believe I'll turn in. Jordanna's taking first shift tomorrow, so I plan to sleep in. If you leave before I wake up, I'll see you at the park tomorrow."

Andie had risen, as well. "Rosalyn, promise you'll tell me if you sense anything I should know about the man who's looking for you—or about Ben," she added thoughtfully.

"If I sense any danger to me, or to you, I'll tell you," Rosalyn promised. "As for Ben, well, he'll tell you everything you need to know. Soon, I think."

"Like what?"

Rosalyn smiled. "In due time, dear. Good night." She brushed a fond kiss across Andie's cheek as she passed her.

Andie knew Rosalyn well enough by now to accept that the older woman would answer questions only if she chose to do so. Acknowledging defeat, she murmured, "Good night. Sleep well."

Preoccupied with her concerns about Rosalyn and her strong attraction to Ben, Andie wasn't sure *she* would sleep at all.

MICK JAGGER screamed unintelligible lyrics into his ear as Ben forced himself to do another five push-ups. Then he collapsed onto the hotel room floor, ripped off the headphones and tossed them on top of the small tape player lying beside him. His breathing was labored, his nearly nude body covered with a glistening layer of sweat, but he doubted that he would sleep if he went back to bed. Five in the morning and he was wide awake. The four and a half hours of sleep he'd managed before he'd awakened almost thirty minutes ago were apparently sufficient for tonight. He'd never required much sleep.

Problem was, what was he supposed to do until it was time to eat breakfast and head back to the theme park? The damned park didn't open for another five hours.

He wasted fifteen minutes fantasizing about several things he'd like to be doing. All of which involved Andie McBride. And then he headed for the shower. A cold one.

He figured that the odds were decidedly slim that Andie would willingly fulfill his fantasies once he told her who he really was and why he was here. He fully intended to tell her the truth sometime today.

This case had become strictly personal to him, and he was going to leave it up to Andie to decide whether she wanted to let her kooky family know her location.

BEN WAS BEGINNING to feel as at home at the park as the employees. He flashed his season pass and waved to the gate attendant as he passed through. Then he roamed the grounds, looking for a rainbow-haired clown with chocolate-brown eyes.

He found her near the petting zoo. In full clown regalia, she waddled around the area, passing out balloons and cheery smiles to delighted children. Ben hung back awhile, watching and enjoying her antics. Just as he was about to step forward, Andie was approached by a slender blond man in a felt fedora, a pale pink shirt, pearl gray pleated slacks and pink-and-gray paisley suspenders. The man was juggling three apples, to the clown's exaggerated admiration.

The juggler—Blake, Ben remembered—was the guy who'd tried to keep him out of the fortune-teller's tent last night, the one who'd watched Andie just a bit too closely. He took another step closer to Andie.

Blake made a big production of tossing the apples high into the air several times before offering one to

Andie with a sweeping bow. She gravely accepted the apple and gave Blake a bright red balloon in return. With a tip of his hat, Blake moved on, whistling a Disney tune between his teeth and greeting park guests on his way.

Ben decided he could really dislike that guy with very little effort.

He approached Andie as soon as she was free of admirers for a moment. "Good morning."

She turned with a start. "Good morning. You're here early. Are you conducting more interviews?"

"No. I want to talk to you. When will you have some free time today?"

"I take a lunch break at two. But I have to be back in my dressing room by three to get ready for the circus performance."

He didn't think an hour would be long enough to fill her in on her family's search for her and his involvement in it. But he didn't want to pass up the chance to have lunch with her, either, so he said, "All right. I'll meet you outside your dressing room at two."

She nodded. "Fine. If you're not going to do any more interviews today, what *are* you going to do?"

"I thought I'd follow you around. Watch how you work."

She frowned, the serious expression an odd contrast to the cheerful makeup. "For your article?"

Wondering how he was going to evade Andie's questions, Ben turned to study the small domesticated animals roaming behind the rail fence of the petting zoo.

Then he stuck his hands into the pockets of his cutoffs and moved toward the gate. "Think I'll go pet a goat," he said.

IT WAS ANOTHER blisteringly hot July day. Though shaded benches were positioned in several places around the park, most of the rides and attractions were, by necessity, open to the full sun. Andie had explained to Ben that the first-aid stations stayed busy with heat-related complaints, despite the ticket takers' warnings to all guests about using precautions against the heat and sun.

"How do you stay cool in all that clown garb and makeup?" Ben asked her, his forehead and upper lip dotted with tiny drops of perspiration, his dark hair damp around his face. "I'm wearing a lightweight shirt and shorts, and I'm sweltering," he added unnecessarily.

Andie made a rueful face and felt the makeup sticking as she did so. "Who said I stay cool? I'm burning up in here. I'm just used to it by now. I have sunscreen in my makeup to protect my skin and the outfit is as loose as I can wear it and still hold it on. I drink a lot of water—through straws, of course," she added with a laugh and a gesture toward her brightly painted mouth, "and I stand in the shade whenever possible, but it's definitely not a cool job. That's why my clown shift only lasts four hours. I couldn't take much more than that. At least I'm not in one of the roving-animal costumes. Now those guys get hot!"

She waved to a six-foot-tall, heavily furred walking bear as she spoke. Surrounded by awed children, the bear—who was really a friendly teenager named Mike—waved back to Andie, calling the children's attention to the clown. Ben stood back as Andie was rapidly surrounded by children wanting to shake her gloved hands.

Andie's shift was almost over when a middle-aged woman in a stylish black blouse and black jeans collapsed almost at Ben's feet. The woman had been waiting while her two young granddaughters visited with Andie. Andie had noticed that the woman looked pale and hot, but had been distracted by the children.

The children squealed. "Nonnie! Something's wrong with our Nonnie!" the older one cried.

Andie moved toward the woman, but Ben was faster. He knelt beside the woman and tested her pulse. "Looks like heat exhaustion," he murmured. "I want to get her out of this sun. You summon the medics."

Andie reached for the small walkie-talkie clipped discreetly to her wide red belt. All park employees were required to carry them for cases like this. While she summoned assistance, Ben lifted the woman easily and carried her to the shade of a nearby tree. Andie could hear him speaking soothingly to the crying children, reassuring them that their Nonnie was fine, just a bit too hot.

A small curious crowd began to gather. Andie efficiently shooed them away. A sidelong glance told her that Ben was fully in charge of the situation. He had loosened the woman's collar and was wiping her face with his handkerchief, which he'd dipped into a cup of ice water provided by a helpful bystander. The woman, who was coming around, was terribly embarrassed by her predicament.

"Hey, don't worry about it," Andie heard Ben say kindly. "It's darned hot today. I'm feeling a little melted myself."

He really was a nice guy, Andie thought as she knelt to comfort the woman's frightened granddaughters. Yet, even though she admired his take-charge competence, it made her all the more wary of her attraction to him. Confident, cocky and utterly masculine—the kind of man who'd probably feel it necessary to take care of his woman—Ben could be a serious threat to her precious newfound independence should they become involved in a relationship.

Andie made a rueful face. What was she thinking? *His woman?* What had gotten into her? One kiss at the top of a Ferris wheel hardly constituted a relationship, even the beginnings of one! *Stop worrying, Andie.*

The medics arrived with a wheelchair for their patient and tiny grinning teddy bears for the children—another park procedure that always seemed to soothe upset youngsters in cases like this. The woman allowed herself to be wheeled to the air-conditioned first-aid station for evaluation and the somewhat soothed children followed behind the wheelchair.

Ben was shaking his head when he walked back to Andie's side. "Wearing hot black clothes on a day like today. Can you believe that?" he muttered. "You'd think a woman her age would know better."

"You were wonderful," Andie said without stopping to think.

Ben's eyes widened at her enthusiastic praise. He might have even blushed a bit, though he was too flushed from the heat and excitement for Andie to be sure. She was grateful again for her clown makeup, since her imprudent words had brought a suspicious warmth to her own cheeks. *Oh, way to go, Andie. Are you looking for trouble or what?*

They stood there staring at each other for a moment. Something flared in Ben's glittering green eyes. Andie was trying to analyze his expression when a sharp tug at one pant leg made her look down. A little boy with a scattering of freckles and two missing teeth grinned up at her. "Hi, clown," he said.

Andie forced a broad smile. "Well, hi! Are you having fun at Big Top?"

Ben stepped back to let her get back to work. But even as Andie slid into her jovial clown routine, she was intensely aware of him standing only a few feet away.

Just what was happening here, anyway? she wondered a bit nervously. Where was this leading?

She found herself suddenly recklessly impatient to find out.

BEN MOVED AWAY from the tree against which he'd been leaning and smiled when Andie rejoined him after changing for lunch. "As much as I like your clown face,

I like this one much better," he said, gently touching her freshly scrubbed and more discreetly made-up cheek.

His touch, slight as it was, sent a ripple of warmth through her. She tried to ignore it as she returned his smile. "Thank you."

He moved his hand to trail his fingers through her shoulder-length near-black curls. "And this is much nicer than the rainbow wig." His smile faded as his eyes locked with hers.

She had to clear her throat before she could speak. "Thank you again," she tried to say lightly, though she knew the effort fell rather flat.

He slid his hands to her waist and drew her closer to him. "And your baggy clown clothes don't begin to do justice to this very nice figure," he murmured, his gaze skimming over her snug pink T-shirt and pastel plaid shorts.

She could feel her breasts tighten beneath his slow appraisal. Her breath wasn't quite steady. "Ben . . ."

She wasn't sure what she would have said. Maybe she'd have chided him for getting too personal or told him he was embarrassing her. Words were forgotten when he lowered his mouth to hers.

As brief as it had been, the kiss at the top of the Ferris wheel the evening before had shaken her. This one rocked her all the way to her toes.

His mouth was firm and demanding, yet infinitely seductive. He slid his hands more firmly around her and pulled her fully into his embrace. Andie thought for only a moment of resisting, then surrendering to her own impulses, she wrapped her arms around his neck and parted her lips in an eager invitation for him to deepen the kiss.

In a flash of total self-honesty she silently admitted that she'd been wanting to do this from the moment she'd bumped into him and felt his warm steadying hands on her shoulders. The time she'd spent with him since had only reinforced her initial attraction to him.

Ben softly groaned his approval of her cooperation. His tongue slipped skillfully between her lips and initiated a leisurely exploration that soon had her trembling against him.

*Dear heaven*, she thought. She didn't know if this man could write, but, oh, could he kiss!

Someone bumped her roughly from behind. She broke the kiss with a gasp, her heart pounding, her knees weak. She stared up at Ben and saw that his expression looked as dazed as her own must be.

"Sorry," a familiar voice said. "I guess I wasn't watching where I was going."

Andie blinked rapidly and tried to regain her composure. She pulled her arms from around Ben's neck and turned. "That's okay, Blake," she said huskily, wishing she could do something about the blush that was working its way up from her collar to the roots of her hair. "We were just going to lunch. Would you like to join us?" she added to be polite.

His handsome face shaded by the ever-present fedora, Blake looked from Andie to Ben before shaking his head. "No, thanks. I've already eaten. You performing with Milo today, Andie?"

"Yes, of course." She glanced at her watch and noticed to her chagrin that her hand was still shaking. "I'd better hurry if I'm going to have time to eat and change for the performance. See you later, Blake."

"Right." He nodded curtly at Ben. "I'll be seeing you, too, Sherman."

Ben muttered something unintelligible. He watched Blake step into the employee building and close the door behind him, then turned back to Andie. "Just how well do you know that guy?" he demanded.

Andie bristled at Ben's tone. She lifted her chin. "He's one of my friends here. Why?"

"There's something about him I don't trust."

"Don't make judgments about people you don't know," she snapped, and turned in the direction of the cafeteria.

Ben caught her arm. "Are you seeing him?"

Her eyes narrowed. "I see him every day."

A muscle twitched in his jaw. "That's not what I meant and you know it. Are you involved with that guy, Andie?"

"If I was, would I have been kissing you just now?" she demanded in exasperation.

"I don't know."

"Well, I wouldn't have been! I don't operate that way."

He nodded in apparent satisfaction. "Good."

"Fine." She pulled her arm out of his loose clasp. "I'm hungry. If you're going to eat with me, you'd better come on."

This time he sounded rather amused when he replied. "Okay, I'm coming, I'm coming."

She could almost have hit him for laughing at her. How dared he make her feel so good one minute and so darned mad the next?

And wasn't this exactly what she'd been worried about—that he'd come into her life and take charge, threatening all the progress she'd made at being independent? She really was going to have to be more careful around this disturbing man, she reminded herself as she hurried toward the safety of the crowded cafeteria.

BEN CONCENTRATED on charming Andie back into a good mood during lunch. He shouldn't have pushed her about Blake, but he'd been jealous, dammit. He couldn't remember the last time he'd been jealous over any woman.

He'd only known Andie for three days. Just what in hell was going on here?

It didn't take him long to have her smiling again. He all but patted himself on the back when she burst out laughing at one of his quips. "You're insane," she told him, pushing her empty lunch plate away.

"Probably," he agreed with a grin. And then he gestured at the costumed circus performers and park employees all around them. "Looks like I fit right in here, don't you think?"

"I suppose you do at that." She glanced at her watch. "I have fifteen minutes before I have to change for the performance. What did you want to talk to me about?"

Ben shook his head. "There's not time for it now. How about later this evening? Have dinner with me— somewhere other than the park," he suggested, thinking of a cozy little place with candlelit tables and mellow background music. After that, if Andie was still speaking to him, maybe they could go dancing or something. Then, well, he could only hope.

She pulled her lower lip between her teeth and the gesture made him long to taste that lip again for himself. He dragged his gaze upward from her mouth to her hesitant eyes. "Did you have other plans for the evening?" he asked reluctantly.

"No."

"Then you'll have dinner with me?"

"Yes," she said with sudden decision, though he didn't understand why she looked so nervous about accepting a simple dinner invitation. "You can pick me up at my place."

"Great. I'll need directions of course," he added, remembering he wasn't supposed to know where she lived.

"Of course. I'll write them down for you."

"Good."

She finished her iced tea and set the empty plastic tumbler beside her plate. "Is there something in particular you want to talk about this evening? Does it have anything to do with the article you're writing?"

"Yes," he said simply. After all, he planned to tell her that there *was* no article. Never had been.

He only hoped she didn't punch him in the mouth when she found out.

Her family owed him for this awkward situation. Damned if he wouldn't send them a whopping bill.

Andie stood and reached for her tray. "I'd better get ready for the circus."

Ben rose and cleared his own dishes. "Good luck on your performance. Or should I say, break a leg?"

"I prefer good luck to broken bones," she answered with a smile. "I never did understand the point of that phrase."

Ben was hoping for a little luck himself. In finding the right words to tell Andie the truth. In persuading her to forgive him for the deception and to understand that it hadn't been his idea. Maybe he'd even be fortunate enough to convince her to give the two of them a chance to find out if there was more between them than simple physical attraction.

It was going to take a lot of luck to accomplish all that in one evening, he thought ruefully. And then he smiled faintly. Luck was his name, after all. Thus far in his thirty-two years it had generally been on his side.

He only hoped it would come through for him again this time.

# 6

LATER THAT AFTERNOON Andie was sawn in half, condensed into an impossibly tiny shape in a box that grew smaller and smaller as Milo took away whole sections at a time, turned into a chicken and made to disappear in a flash of smoke. All of which she found preferable to wearing the spike heels that were an obligatory part of her costume. Back in her dressing room, she pried them off with her usual gusty sigh of relief.

Across the dressing room, a large woman in the baggy flowered dress of a clown pulled a frizzy red wig from her head and laughed. "You always make that same sound when you take off those shoes, Andie, did you know that?"

"I know," Andie admitted ruefully. "Lord, I hate these things."

"So how come you wear them?" the clown asked logically, taking off her own big floppy unlaced boots.

"'Cause she wants her legs to look sexy, of course," Polly, the bosomy blond equestrian, said as her head emerged from the tight T-shirt that had replaced her own spangled costume. "Right, Andie?"

Andie made a face. "I suppose. Though I don't know why a magician's assistant has to look sexy."

"To distract the audience, of course. If they're busy looking at your legs, they aren't watching Milo's sleight of hand."

Andie laughed. "That's what Milo keeps telling me. Talk about a sexist rationale . . ."

Polly shrugged matter-of-factly. "Doesn't bother me to wear my little spangled leotards. I like looking good. And, besides, haven't you ever watched the women in the audience when Glenn and Tony flex all those muscles before they start their trapeze act? It's the same thing."

"What a waste of prime male flesh," Mildred, the heavy clown, muttered with a regretful sigh as she scrubbed makeup from her pleasantly plain face.

"Speaking of prime male flesh," Polly said, taking a few steps closer to Andie, who sat on a low bench tying her running shoes, "what about that guy who's been following you around the park the past couple of days? He's gorgeous."

Ben's wickedly handsome face immediately flashed through Andie's mind. "Yes, I suppose he is at that," she murmured.

"So who is he? There's a rumor he's a magazine writer doing an article about the park."

"That's true. He's supposed to be talking to several park employees. Hasn't he interviewed you yet?"

"No," Polly said regretfully, "he hasn't."

"Me, either," Mildred piped in as she buttoned a man's plaid shirt over her jeans. "Darn it."

Andie frowned. "Odd. How about you, Cassie?" she asked a striking raven haired woman in a sleek satin pants outfit who'd just entered the dressing room. "Have you been interviewed for an article about the park yet?"

The animal trainer shook her head. "No. I've heard someone's doing one, but no one's contacted me yet. Is it the cute guy you've been hanging around with?"

"Yes," Andie admitted slowly, wondering who, besides her, Ben *had* interviewed during the past three days.

"I think our reporter has gotten distracted from his article," Polly mused speculatively, her heavily madeup eyes sparkling with mischief. "I think he's turning his article into an in-depth interview with a certain clown-slash-magician's assistant. I saw him watching her during the circus performance. Wish he'd have paid as much attention to *my* act!"

Mildred grinned. "Now that you mention it, I *wondered* if kissing at the top of the Ferris wheel was a standard interview technique. Hell, I was about to volunteer to tell the guy anything he wanted to know."

Andie's cheeks warmed. "You saw that?" she asked weakly.

"No, Puck did," Mildred replied, naming the young man who usually operated the Ferris wheel. "He told Cal, who told Mitch, who told R.J., who—"

"Okay, I get the picture," Andie muttered. "Damn, you guys are nosy." Which seemed odd, considering the usual carnie tendency toward privacy within the ranks.

*Just Her Luck*

Cassie sat in front of a brightly lit mirror removing the skillfully applied makeup that took at least ten years off her age, which Andie had estimated to be close to forty. She was still an attractive woman, not classically beautiful, but exotically intriguing. Though Cassie tended to be a bit distant, Andie liked her and enjoyed Cassie's sharp dry wit. "Everyone's just a little concerned about you, Andie," she said unexpectedly, without looking away from the mirror. "You've only just met this man, after all. For all you know, he could be married or something."

"He wouldn't be the first to lie about that," Polly said with a bitterness that spoke of painful experience.

Mildred sighed her agreement. "Or maybe he's one of those weirdos who likes to wear your underwear. I met this guy once who—"

"I can't believe this," Andie said, throwing up her hands in exasperation. "I thought carnies had this thing about giving each other privacy."

Cassie half turned on her stool. "Carnies take care of their own," she said, then made a rueful face at the corny comment.

"I can take care of myself," Andie replied, though their concern touched her. "Please don't worry about me."

"You're the baby in the bunch," Polly said with a smile. "We can't help ourselves."

"I'm not a baby! I'm twenty-five years old!"

Polly, Mildred and Cassie groaned in unison and shared an envious look. Mildred was the one who finally spoke. "You just be careful, kid. Like the song says, there ain't nothing sadder than the tears of a clown." She grinned at her own wit.

Andie couldn't help laughing softly. "You guys are all nuts. But thanks for caring."

"So you'll be careful?" Polly asked a bit too casually.

"I'll be careful," Andie answered firmly.

"Good."

Cassie turned back to the mirror. "Blake's out in the hallway, Andie. He said he wants to talk to you."

Andie swallowed a groan. Not Blake, too. How had she gotten herself adopted by this sweet unexpectedly overprotective bunch? She really wasn't the youngest employee at the park. There were dozens of teenagers working the midway and the music shows. Why couldn't these nice meddlers pick one of them to mother?

"All right, I'm on my way out. See you guys Wednesday." Tuesday was Andie's day off, since no park employee could put in more than five and a half days a week.

Still immaculate in his pink and gray, even after a day of roaming the park, Blake leaned carelessly against the grubby wall of the hallway, lazily flipping an open pocketknife from hand to hand. Andie winced as the flashing sharp-looking blade came dangerously close to his palm and wondered if his hands were ever still. "You wanted to talk to me?"

He tossed the knife high in the air, hardly glanced at it as he caught it easily, then spun it again. "Yeah."

"Would you mind putting that away first? I'd just as soon not lose any toes during our conversation."

He grinned, but obediently caught the knife, closed it and stuffed it into the right front pocket of his loose-fitting slacks. "I never cut off toes by accident," he assured her.

"I can't tell you how reassuring that is. Now, what was it you wanted to discuss?"

Blake's expression grew serious. "It's about this guy who's been hanging around you . . ."

Andie swallowed a groan. "What about him?" she asked in resignation.

"What magazine did he tell you he's writing for?"

She shrugged. "He didn't mention the name. I assumed he's working free-lance. Why?"

"I happened to get my hands on the letter he sent to Parker, setting up this research trip—"

"How did you manage that?"

He ignored her question. "I called some of the magazines he listed as references—or, at least, the two of five he listed that actually exist. They've never heard of a writer named Ben Sherman."

Andie felt something cold and hard settle in the pit of her stomach. "What are you saying? That he's a fake?"

Blake only looked at her.

She shook her head. "Why would he lie about his job? He's studied every inch of this park, asked a hundred questions, taken lots of notes. Why would he do that, unless he really is writing an article?"

"Good question. Why *would* he do that? And why would he only be interested in interviewing you?"

Andie's hands had gone icy. She clenched them together in front of her, trying to warm them. "You must have made a mistake. Mr. Parker wouldn't be so careless. Surely Ben enclosed sample articles with the letter."

"Two," Blake said. "Neither of them had bylines so I checked with the magazines. He didn't write either of them."

Damn. Damn, damn, *damn!* "There has to be a mistake," she repeated flatly, unable to accept that Ben had been lying to her from the first. She thought of that sweet kiss they'd shared on the Ferris wheel and the more passionate one outside this very building before lunch. Had the kisses been lies, too? What could Ben possibly hope to gain by getting friendly with her? Unless . . .

She thought of his questions about Rosalyn, his apparent dislike of her sweet housemate. What if . . . ?

"Oh, my God," she whispered.

Blake reached out quickly to take her arm. "Hey! You okay? You've gone white as a sheet."

"I'm fine," she whispered through dry lips. "Just . . . give me a minute."

"Take all the time you need. As long as you're taking me seriously."

"I am," she murmured. She was taking him very seriously.

"Good."

"What am I going to do now?" she murmured, more to herself than to Blake.

He answered, anyway. "Let me handle it," he offered. "A couple of the guys and I will have a little talk with this Sherman, find out what he wants, let him know what we think about jerks who try to con us. He won't bother you again when we get through with him."

"No!" Andie said quickly—a bit too quickly. It worried her how intensely she hated the thought of Ben being hurt, even after finding out that he'd probably lied to her. And yet, she reminded herself with feeble optimism, she still didn't know for sure that Ben wasn't exactly what he'd said he was. Blake could be wrong. She had to find out for herself.

"He's supposed to be waiting outside for me," she said disconsolately.

Blake adjusted his fedora. "Okay, let's go."

"No." She placed a restraining hand on his arm. "I'll go. You stay."

"Andie—"

"I mean it, Blake. I can handle this. We'll be out in the open, after all, within sight and hearing of lots of people. I'll find out what's going on, and if I think there's any reason to be concerned, I'll tell you. Okay?"

Blake was scowling. "I don't like this."

"You don't have to. But thank you for being concerned." She felt as though she'd been saying that a lot today. It was nice to have people who cared about her, but . . .

Blake nodded and stepped back. "You know what you're doing, I guess."

She smiled gratefully. "Yes, I do." Or at least she hoped she did. She glanced toward the building exit, cleared her throat, lifted her chin and took a deep breath for courage. She was ready to find out the truth.

She only hoped the truth wouldn't break her heart.

BEN WAS STARTING to feel quite proprietary about the big oak tree outside the park employee building. He'd waited here for Andie so often that it was becoming his tree. And now that they'd shared one mind-blowing kiss beneath it, he liked it even more.

One shoulder comfortably planted against the time-worn trunk, he glanced at his watch for the third time in almost as many minutes. What was keeping Andie? She knew he was waiting for her out here.

He was impatient to be with her again, and they'd been separated less than two hours. The very depth of that impatience made him frown. This thing between them was moving too fast, getting too intense, he thought warily. Last time he'd felt this way about any woman had been back in college, when he'd thought himself in love with the fraternity sweetheart. He'd thought she loved him, too, until he'd discovered that she took her title as fraternity sweetheart a bit too liberally. To his disappointment, he'd learned that several of his fraternity brothers knew his lover as intimately as he did. She hadn't even bothered to be particularly discreet about it.

Paula's infidelity hadn't permanently put him off relationships, but in the ensuing years he'd been careful about falling too hard or too fast—until he'd met Andie and instantly forgotten every scrap of the caution he'd exercised during his adulthood.

It wasn't smart to let himself feel this way about a woman to whom he'd been lying from the first time he'd spoken to her. Problem was, it was too late to do anything about it now. He could only hope she'd understand—eventually.

A door opened and Andie stepped out. His pulse leaping in response, Ben moved forward eagerly to greet her.

Her grim expression stopped him in his tracks.

She stood several feet away from him, her purple tote slung over one shoulder, her arms crossed at her waist in an obvious don't-get-close posture. "What magazine did you say you're working for, Ben?"

*Oh, hell.* He cleared his throat. "I . . . don't think I said."

"Suppose you do so now. Maybe I'll recognize it."

"I don't think you will."

Her mouth twisted. "No. I suppose I wouldn't." She dropped her arms and started past him.

"Hey!" Startled, he reached out to her. She deftly avoided his hand. "Where are you going?" he asked.

"Home."

"You haven't given me directions yet," he reminded her. "What time do you want me to pick you up for dinner?"

"I don't."

He drew a deep breath for patience. "You want to tell me what's going on here? I seem to be a few steps behind."

She turned on him then, her dark eyes snapping furiously. "You lied to me, didn't you? There is no article."

"I..." He gestured ineffectually with one hand, caught off guard by her accuracy. How had she found out, dammit? He'd wanted to break the truth to her in his own way. "Andie..."

She must have read the answer in his eyes. Her shoulders sagged for a moment as though in bitter disappointment, and then squared fiercely. "I don't know what you're after, but I want you to stay away from me, is that clear?" she asked icily. "If there's one thing I detest, it's a liar."

"Andie, listen to me."

"I've wasted enough time listening to you. Why should I waste more, when nothing you say is true, anyway? I have things to do," she said, turning away from him with every indication that she'd said all she intended to say. Ever.

Frustrated, he reached out and his fingers closed over her arm before she could evade him this time. "Andie, would you just—"

*"Don't touch me!"* There was fear in her voice, and in her eyes when she looked wildly over her shoulder at him.

Sickened by the look on her face, he immediately dropped his hand.

"Get away from her. Now!"

The angrily growled command came from Blake, who stood behind them, his fists clenched at his sides. A hairy six-foot-five three-hundred-pound man in a stretched-to-the-limit park employee T-shirt loomed behind him. Ben felt the neck of his own shirt grow suddenly tight around his throat. "I wasn't going to hurt her."

"Damn straight you're not," the big man snarled.

"Blake, I told you I'd handle this," Andie said. "Please take Tiny and go. Ben was just leaving, weren't you, Ben?" she said meaningfully.

Tiny? Ben glanced warily at the threatening mountain. "Andie, I need to talk to you," he said carefully. "Blake can stay if it makes you feel safer, though I promise you I would never hurt you."

"You already have," she whispered, her dark eyes suddenly liquid. "You lied to me. Why?"

"I didn't want to," he said, desperately trying to make her understand. "But I'd made a promise—"

"A promise? To whom?" she asked suspiciously.

"Your family," he answered in resignation. "Your parents, Nolan and Gladys McBride. Your brother-in-law, Donald the dentist, and your sister, Gloria. Even your grandmother thought it best for me to approach you carefully. I think she was afraid you'd move again if you knew your family had found you."

Andie looked stunned. "My family sent you to find me?"

He nodded grimly. "They were worried about you. I tried to tell them I didn't want to lie to you, but they wouldn't listen. To my regret, I let them talk me into going along with them. I'm sorry. I should have handled this my own way."

"My family never listens to anyone," Andie murmured, still looking at him skeptically. "You swear you're telling the truth now? Your presence here has nothing to do with Rosalyn? You don't mean her any harm?"

"Your grandmother told me you were mixed up with a psychic," Ben admitted. "Other than that, I know absolutely nothing about Rosalyn—and, no, I have no intention of harming her, or anyone else, for that matter."

"Wait a minute," Blake muttered, moving closer. "What's going on here? Who the hell are you?"

Andie sighed, her acceptance of the truth mirrored in her rueful expression. "He works for my family, Blake. He wasn't tracking down a story. He was tracking me."

Blake frowned at Ben. "You a cop? A PI?"

"An insurance-fraud investigator," Ben explained.

Looking startled, Blake glanced quickly at Andie. "Insurance fraud?"

Andie shook her head and held up both hands to protest her innocence. "I don't know anything about insurance fraud!"

"Finding you had nothing to do with my job," Ben assured her quickly. "I was doing this as a favor for my mother."

Andie only looked more confused. "A favor for your mother?"

Damn, but he'd made a mess of this, Ben thought disgustedly. "Well, yeah. You see, she called and—"

"Just who *is* your mother?"

"Jessie Luck." He said the name on a sigh, already predicting her reaction.

Andie winced, then groaned. "Oh."

Since a lot of people reacted that way to hearing his mother's name, Ben wasn't offended. As much as he adored her, he was well aware that his mother was a fruitcake. Most people who knew her couldn't help loving her, but were just a bit wary of her. As Andie apparently was.

"You're Benjamin Luck," she said suddenly, slapping a hand against her head. "You live in Portland."

"My mother's mentioned me, I guess."

"A few times. Dammit, Ben, why didn't you just tell me who you were from the beginning?"

"I've already explained that I promised your family—"

"Oh, bull," she cut in inelegantly. "If you've met my family, you know they're all totally nuts, all except my grandmother. Why would you go along with anything they asked of you? How much are they paying you, anyway?"

"Expenses."

"I don't understand. Why would your mother ask you to find me as a favor to her? And why would you do so for nothing more than expenses?"

"You know my mother. Have you ever tried to tell her no when she asked for anything? I might as well try to stop time from passing."

"I suppose you have some proof of who you are?" Blake wanted to know.

Ben reached for his wallet.

Andie shook her head. "That's not necessary. I believe him, Blake."

"Why?" Blake demanded.

She sighed. "Because I do know Jessie Luck. This sounds exactly like something she and my family would cook up together." She reached out to touch Blake's arm. "I left home several months ago because I needed to get away from my smotheringly overprotective family. I should have known they wouldn't let me go that easily. Thank you for being concerned, Blake, but this really is a personal matter now. I can handle it from here."

Ben scowled at the ease with which she touched the other man, the sincerity of her smile for him. Dammit, she'd looked at *him* like he was an ax murderer!

Blake didn't appear particularly satisfied by Andie's explanation. "You're going to let him get away with lying to you—to all of us?"

"I said I can handle it from here," Andie repeated more firmly. "I didn't say I was letting him get away with anything."

Ben managed not to wince at the seething anger audible in her voice. This wasn't going to be pretty, he thought in resignation. There was a good chance he was going to have to grovel before it was over, and he'd always been lousy at groveling.

Blake studied Andie's face for a moment and finally seemed satisfied with what he found there. He nodded abruptly. "All right. As you said, this is your business. I'll stay out of it. But if you need me, if the guy harasses you or anything, you just let me know, okay?"

"Or me," Tiny put in. It was obvious he was more than a little disappointed that there wasn't going to be any trouble at the moment.

Ben exhaled in relief that Andie hadn't asked her enormous champion to attack first and ask questions later. He hadn't forgotten the last little favor he'd done for one of his mother's friends. He'd gone to pull a rebellious teenager out of a biker bar, and the bar patrons hadn't been pleased with his interference into their lives. He'd been lucky to get out with all his teeth. For several weeks afterward, he'd looked as though he'd had a close encounter with a cement truck. He didn't particularly relish the thought of looking that way again—and Tiny looked capable of doing about as much damage as three ordinary-size bikers.

Andie gave Tiny a smile as bright and affectionate as the ones she gave the kids who hung around her when she was in her clown costume. "Thank you, Tiny. It's sweet of you to offer, but everything's fine now. I'll let you go back to work."

Sweet? Ben watched in astonishment as the big man blushed brightly behind his shaggy brown beard, mumbled something unintelligible and lumbered away with one last ominous glare at Ben. Blake followed, though he, too, gave Ben a long, assessing vaguely warning look before leaving.

Ben ran his tongue across his nice straight teeth in silent celebration that they'd escaped harm once again. Then he turned back to Andie. "Where can we talk?"

"We can't," she said flatly. The smile she'd given Tiny had vanished without a trace. "Goodbye, Ben. Tell my family I'm fine, and I'll call them when I'm ready to talk to them. *If* I ever talk to any of them again after this!"

"Come on, Andie, they were worried about you. Surely you can understand that. And why are you still so angry with me? You don't really blame me for your family's actions, do you?"

"Blame you?" she repeated incredulously. "Why am I angry with you?"

She took one step toward him, her furious eyes locked with his, her slender body quivering with rage. For a moment Ben thought she might hit him. Andie McBride had quite a temper, he'd learned during the past three days. Even now, when he should be thinking of new ways to apologize to her, he couldn't help wondering if all her passions were as volatile.

"Let me tell you why I'm angry with you, Ben Sherman...er, Benjamin Luck, since you're apparently too dense to figure it out for yourself."

He winced and started to protest, but she overrode him. "You've lied to me from the first word you said to me," she said from between clenched teeth. "You yelled at my housemate for no good reason. You spied on me without my knowledge and against my will. You've humiliated me in front of my coworkers. And you've probably cost me a job I love, because I'm quite sure Parker will fire me when he finds out that you used him and the park to get to me. *That's* why I'm angry with you. And that's why I never want to see you again!"

She really was spectacular in full temper. And she had every reason to be mad at him. Everything she'd said was true—with one exception. "You won't lose your job," he promised her. "I sent my notes to a friend who publishes a travel magazine. He's interested in featuring the park in a future issue. He's going to send a real writer to get a few more details—and a photographer. Parker's going to love it. He won't ever have to know why I was really here."

"Good," she said without enthusiasm. "At least I'm spared that mortification. Now if you'll excuse me, I have things to do. Goodbye."

"This isn't goodbye, Andie."

She refused to argue. Instead, she pointedly turned her back and stalked away.

Ben didn't try to follow her. She needed the time to cool down.

There was always tomorrow.

# 7

"HAVE YOU FOUND HER, Benji?"

"I found her," Ben answered his mother over the telephone Tuesday morning. "And don't call me Benji," he added automatically, after years of futilely protesting the despised nickname.

"Is she all right?"

"She's fine. She's happy here. Tell her family there is absolutely no reason to be concerned about her." He made the statement firmly, refusing to dwell on his own concern that Andie had somehow gotten herself involved in something dangerous, something that had to do with her so-called psychic housemate.

"Oh." Jessie didn't sound convinced. "But what about that strange psychic person Maybelle was so concerned about?"

"A harmless middle-aged lady who makes her living telling people what they want to hear," Ben replied, hoping he was telling the truth.

"What a relief. I guess Maybelle read incorrectly between the lines of Andie's letters."

"I guess she did."

"So Andie still thinks you're writing a travel article?"

"No," Ben answered bluntly. "She found out the truth. I told you she would."

"Oh, dear. Is she very much annoyed with you?"

"She wants my liver. On a platter. She probably wouldn't mind having yours and every member of her family's as a side dish."

"Really, Benjamin, how distasteful."

"That's probably tame compared to what she's *really* thinking. No one bothered to warn me that Andie McBride has a hair-trigger temper."

*"Andie?"* Now Jessie sounded utterly bewildered. "I've known that child for nearly thirteen years and I've never seen her lose her temper. Are you sure you have the right woman?"

Ben didn't bother to respond to that inane question. "Trust me, she has a temper."

"You must have done something to annoy her."

Ben bit his tongue to keep from yelling at his mother that he was taking the brunt of Andie's temper through no fault of his own; that it was Jessie's idea, and Andie's family's, for him to sneak around undercover for this particular assignment. Sure, it had come naturally to him. He went undercover often enough on his job, had told enough lies to embarrass the devil himself, but that was work. This had been personal. He should have known better than to mix the two.

"Look, I've got to go," he said abruptly. "Just tell the McBrides that Andie's okay, will you?"

"Are you very angry with me, Benji?" his mother asked in a small voice.

Ben sighed and softened, just as he always did in response to that wounded tone. "No, Mother, I'm not angry. I just wish I'd handled this differently, that's all."

"Oh. Do you like Andie?"

"Yeah. But she doesn't particularly like me."

"Oh, that's all right," Jessie said, suddenly happy again. "She'll come around quickly enough. They always do when my boys turn on the charm. Look at how quickly Jonathan won Amanda's heart. Just like your father, both of you. Oh, Ben, this is wonderful. My sons both married to daughters of my dear friends."

"*Married?*" Ben repeated in a choked voice. "Mother—"

"Goodbye, darling. You'll let me know how it all works out." It wasn't a question.

"Mother—" But Ben was talking to a dial tone. He scrubbed a hand over his face and muttered a few blistering curses that he never would have said in his mother's presence. Honestly, the woman was impossible. If he didn't love her so much, he'd probably see about having her committed.

"Married," he grumbled with a snort. "Hah! I hardly even know Andie. She won't even speak to me, and Mother's talking marriage. What a joke."

But he wasn't smiling as he dialed his brother's home number in Seattle. He hoped Jon hadn't yet left for his work in the homicide division of the Seattle police department. He was relieved when Jon answered the phone. "It's Ben. Did you find out anything about Carmody or Milo?"

"Hello to you, too, little brother. My family and I are fine, thank you. And you?"

Ben winced at the sarcasm in his brother's deep voice. "Sorry. Guess I was a little abrupt, wasn't I?"

"A bit. Problems?"

"Nothing I can't handle."

"Seems like I've heard this before."

"Jon . . ." Ben growled impatiently.

"Okay, the answer is no. I can't find any priors on either of them. That doesn't mean they haven't done anything—only that they haven't been charged or convicted, not in this country, anyway."

"I understand. Thanks for trying."

"Want me to do some further checking?"

"Yeah, if you've got time. Something strange is going on here—I just wish to hell I knew what it is. Carmody's scared of something, and Andie's terrified for her. I think it might be something more than a simple con."

"You be careful, Ben."

"You can bet on it. You have my number if you come up with anything."

"Right."

Ben hung up with a hollow feeling of dread. Was it because he had to face Andie—and her temper—again soon? Or was it something more serious? Ben intended to find out what it was that Andie and her housemate were hiding. Soon. For his own peace of mind.

BEN HAD BEEN through the entire park twice searching for Andie before someone finally told him it was Andie's day off. Cursing beneath his breath, he wiped his brow with the back of one wrist and headed grimly for the exit.

He drove straight to her house, where he stood on her porch and pounded on the door for a full fifteen minutes before finally conceding that she wasn't home. Where the hell was she, anyway?

He had a sudden sick feeling that she was gone. That her family's discovery of her whereabouts had made her run again. Would she have packed up and left during the night? *Would he ever see her again?*

And then he forced himself to slow down and think rationally. Andie loved it here. She loved her job, her friends, her housemate. She wouldn't just pick up and leave.

Would she?

Twenty minutes later Ben pushed through the beads of the fortune-teller's tent. Two teenage girls, holding numbered slips of paper in their hands, sat in the waiting area, whispering and giggling. Dammit, Ben thought impatiently, why didn't they just go ride a roller coaster or something?

The bored-looking blond girl was back behind the counter, dressed as before in a yellow caftan. "Take a number," she said, without looking up from the fashion magazine spread out in front of her.

"No," Ben said, "I'm not taking a number. I have to ask Rosalyn something as soon as she's free."

The girl looked up, frowning a bit. Her heavily mascaraed eyes widened in recognition. "You're Andie's friend, aren't you?"

For all Andie's talk about privacy among the employees here, gossip sure seemed to travel fast, Ben reflected as he nodded. "Yeah."

"Rosalyn's with someone right now."

He moved around the counter. "I'll wait."

Almost as the words left his mouth, a woman came through the back curtain into the waiting room, her expression thoughtful. Without hesitating, Ben crossed the room with determined steps.

"Hey!" one of the teenage girls protested. "We're next."

"I'll just be a minute," Ben assured her. "She's my grandmother."

"Oh." Mollified, the girls settled back in their chairs. Their gazes moved with interest over Ben's bare tanned legs as he entered the fortune-teller's room.

"Your grandmother, Benjamin?" Rosalyn asked reprovingly from the chair behind the little table. "I don't really think I'm quite that old."

"It was all I could think of to say," he said with an unapologetic shrug. "Where's Andie?"

She lifted a brow at the curt question. "Today is her day off."

"I know. She's not at home. Where is she?"

"What makes you think Andie gives me a full itinerary of her free time?"

"Look, can't you just let me have a straight answer for once? Do you know where Andie is or not?"

"Sit down a moment, please, Ben."

He sighed. "I didn't come to have my fortune told."

"Please."

Her eyes never wavered as he attempted to stare her down. He finally gave up and plopped into the chair. "I suppose you want to hold my hand again."

She bit her lip against a smile. "If you don't mind."

He held out his hand with a long-suffering expression. "Is this going to help you find Andie? Behind someone's dresser, perhaps?"

She clucked reprovingly and shook her silvery head. "You aren't in a very good mood today, are you, dear?"

He had the grace to squirm and say, "Sorry. I guess I'm not."

"That's quite all right," she said kindly. "We all have bad moods at times. Now . . ."

By this time he was accustomed to the slight tingling in his palm as her fingers closed around his. He still didn't much like it.

"Andie's very angry with you."

"You don't have to read my mind to know that. She probably told you all about it last night."

Rosalyn chuckled. "Yes. I don't believe I've ever seen her quite so passionate."

Ben nearly choked at the word, and the immediate powerful longing to redirect Andie's passions in another direction.

Rosalyn's violet eyes became serious. "I don't want you to hurt her, Benjamin. Andie has become very dear to me. She's a strong, brave, loving, generous young woman. She's also extremely loyal—unlike the flighty girl you thought yourself in love with before."

She was doing it again, dammit. He pulled his hand from hers, and she made no effort to restrain him. "I have no intention of hurting Andie," he said, ignoring Rosalyn's reference to his past. "I only want to find her and apologize again for deceiving her."

"You're afraid she's in danger."

"The thought has crossed my mind," he admitted evenly.

"Yes. You're more than a bit intuitive yourself. Are you aware of that?"

"I don't believe in that garbage."

"No. Of course you don't." Her smile made him uncomfortable. And then she grew serious again. "I'm worried about her, too, Ben. It's . . . not safe for her to be with me."

Ben straightened abruptly. "Then why—?"

"She won't leave me," Rosalyn broke in before he could finish the question. "Once she learned about my troubles, she became even more determined to stay with me. She's protecting me, you see."

"From what?" Ben asked in frustration.

"From a man who wants to kill me. A man who has killed before and wouldn't think twice about hurting Andie or anyone else who gets between him and me."

Ben's stomach clenched in reaction to the ugly words said in such a gentle sweet-sounding voice. "Who is he?"

Rosalyn sighed. "Two years ago police in California enlisted my help in a desperate attempt to solve a series of vicious rapes that had resulted in the deaths of two of the victims. We tried to keep my involvement secret, but a reporter found out and printed the information I had been able to provide with my gift. Apparently my insights were all too accurate. I started receiving threatening letters. And then someone tried to run me down with a car. Had I not sensed danger and jumped out of the way at the last moment, I would have been killed."

Ben winced. "Damn."

"Yes."

"They never caught the guy?"

"No. But the rapes suddenly stopped. I began to feel safe, and then someone shot at me as I left a supermarket one morning."

Ben's hand tightened convulsively on his knee. The thought of someone trying to shoot this harmless woman made him oddly furious. "Were you injured?"

"I wasn't. But an innocent bystander was seriously wounded," Rosalyn said sadly. "The police weren't even sure the shot was meant for me. I knew it was. It was him—and I knew he wouldn't stop until I was dead. He had transferred all that aggression to me, you see. I'm a threat to him. I've become his mission. As long as he is alive and free, I can never be safe. So I ran. Twice

during the past two years he has found me and come
very close to catching me. Both times I've escaped only
at the last minute. I'm afraid there will come a time
when my intuition won't be enough to save me."

Ben wasn't quite sure he believed a word of this—and
he refused to accept that she really was psychic—but
he felt compelled to ask, "If you know who he is, why
haven't the police caught him?"

"But I don't know who he is. I've sensed many things
about him, but not enough to positively identify him,
I'm afraid."

"What *do* you know about him?"

"He's in his thirties. He has a fair complexion—he
may be blond. He came from a troubled home, suffered horrible abuses in childhood. He's brilliant with
numbers. In fact, he's obsessed with them, convinced
that there are lucky numbers and unlucky numbers and
so on. His attacks are probably arranged according to
specific dates or times—some number of special sig-
nificance to him. He's very patient and will wait days
or even months for just the right time, in his own mind,
to make his moves. And somewhere on his body there
is a tattoo that has some meaning for him that no one
else knows."

"That's what was printed in the newspaper article?"

"Yes."

"And you think it's accurate enough that he feels
threatened by it."

"Yes."

"Didn't any of his surviving victims get a look at him?"

"No. He always wore long-sleeved shirts and a ski mask. He, er, unzipped his trousers during the assaults, but he never fully undressed. He never spoke. The victims can say only that he was of average height and weight and that he was very strong."

Ben frowned. "When you collapsed Sunday, you said something about sensing that he was very close. Were you talking about this man?"

"Oh, dear. Did I say that?"

"Yes. Is that what you meant?"

Rosalyn made a fluttery gesture with one hand. "For a moment . . . I thought I felt him. Somewhere nearby. Even watching me, perhaps. There was such hatred . . . such malevolence." She shivered, and her face had gone pale. But then she shook her head and spoke in a firmer tone. "But when I recovered the feeling was gone. It hasn't returned."

"Does that mean he isn't anywhere around here?"

"I wish I could reassure you that he isn't," she murmured, looking worried. "But I can't. My gift isn't that reliable, especially when I am personally involved. But there's something about Andie . . ."

His fist tightened. "What about Andie?"

"A bad feeling. I'm very worried about her, Ben."

"Now? You think she's in danger now?" He was already half out of the chair. He still didn't believe in this malarkey, but if there was even a possibility that Andie was in trouble . . .

"No." Rosalyn reached out to touch his arm soothingly. "Not now." She seemed distracted for a moment, then continued. "She's fine now. She's doing some shopping at the new mall outside of town. But..."

"But...?"

"She will be in danger, I'm afraid," Rosalyn said heavily. "Because of me. I don't know when or how exactly, but I sense that the time will come. I want so badly to stop it. I hope you can help me with that."

"You could leave again," Ben said bluntly. "Move away from her."

Rosalyn nodded, unoffended by the suggestion. "Yes. And if I thought that would protect her, I would do it without hesitation. But I'm not sure it will. He'll find out, you see, that we shared a house. And he'll think she knows where I am. I know you don't believe in my gift, Benjamin, but please try to understand that something drew me to this place several months ago. A feeling that I must be here, that my future would be settled here. I think Andie may have been drawn here by a similar feeling. That worries me of course."

Ben ran a hand through his hair. Why couldn't any of his mother's little favors be simple ones? Running an errand, filing her tax return, fixing a leak in her pipes? Something safe, sane and simple. "Look, Rosalyn—"

"Rosalyn?" The receptionist leaned into the room, looking a bit harried. "You're getting quite a line out here. And they're starting to get restless."

"Thank you, Pam. You may send in the next visitor. I really must get back to work, Ben," Rosalyn said. "Please excuse me now."

"But—"

"You'll find Andie at the mall. Take her to lunch. Beg her forgiveness if necessary. Just help me protect her."

The two teenagers who'd been waiting in the reception room entered with sidelong looks of resentment at Ben. Surrendering, he told Rosalyn firmly that he'd talk to her again later, and then he left.

What the hell, he thought as he climbed into his car. He might as well check out the mall. Rosalyn had probably known all along that Andie was there. She'd just wanted to have a little fun with him first.

But it hadn't been fun at all listening to her unsettling tale of rapes and attempted murder. If any of it was true, if that crazy woman had gotten Andie involved in something this deadly, well, Ben didn't know what he'd do. But he'd do something.

Andie wasn't going to be harmed while he was around to prevent it!

ANDIE LINGERED outside the glitter-filled window of a jewelry store, admiring an expensive delicately wrought diamond-and-sapphire bracelet. Her budget didn't run to such extravagances, but like most women, she loved the sparkle of diamonds.

"It would look beautiful on you," a familiar low voice murmured close to her ear.

She turned her head to find Ben watching her soberly and hoped he couldn't tell how glad she was to see him. She almost reached out to touch him but, instead, curled her fingers more tightly around the paper bookstore bag in her hand. "How did you know where to find me?"

"Rosalyn. You told her you'd be here, didn't you?"

"No," she said honestly, "I didn't. But it doesn't surprise me that she knew."

Ben shook his head. "Now don't start that psychic stuff again. I've had enough of that this morning."

"Rosalyn been telling your future again, Ben?" She tried to remember that she was angry with him, tried to force her lips into a frown, but she couldn't seem to stop smiling.

"No. She's been telling me her past."

The urge to smile vanished abruptly. "She told you everything?"

"Yes. If it's true—"

"It's true!" she cut in heatedly, offended for her friend's sake. "Rosalyn doesn't lie."

"If it's true," he repeated firmly, "then you shouldn't be sharing a house with her. You could be putting yourself in danger."

"And what am I supposed to do, Ben? Move out? Leave her to fend for herself just to make sure I'm safe? What kind of friend would that make me?"

"A smart one. A healthy one."

"A false one. I'd never abandon someone I care for."

A shopper bumped against Ben, apologized and moved on. Ben looked around with a frown. "Is there someplace here where we can have lunch? I'm hungry."

"Has anyone ever pointed out that you have an insatiable appetite?" she asked dryly.

His eyes grew suddenly devilish. "As a matter of fact . . ."

Before he could make the embarrassing innuendo she knew was coming, she hastily stepped away. "There's a pretty good restaurant upstairs. We can eat there."

"Sounds great. Lead the way."

It was only after they'd stepped onto the escalator that Andie realized how easily he'd just manipulated her into having lunch with him.

# 8

A WAITRESS in black slacks and a red-and-white striped shirt took their orders, brought their salads and then left them alone at the small table tucked into a cozy corner of the restaurant. "All right, Ben," Andie said, leaning toward him with a stern expression. "Let's get this over with. Why are you really here in Texas?"

"Nice of you to finally give me a chance to tell my side of the story," he said dryly, picking up his salad fork. He figured he could eat and talk at the same time. He hadn't been exaggerating to Andie before. He really was hungry.

Very matter-of-factly he told her about his mother's telephone call, about his visit with Andie's family, about how reluctant her grandmother had been to reveal Andie's place of employment. He explained how easy it had been to set up his cover story, how he'd automatically slid into undercover habits despite his reluctance to do so this time.

"I never thought Grandma would tell them where I am," Andie said, sounding a bit hurt.

"I don't think she would have if you hadn't worried her with your hints that Rosalyn is in some sort of trouble," Ben answered with a shrug. "Your grandmother seems to be the stubborn type."

Andie's face softened with a fond smile. "Yes. She's always been my link to sanity in the middle of my family."

Ben thought about his confrontation with the eccentric McBrides and suppressed a shudder. "I can understand that. Your sister thinks you need to be deprogrammed, by the way. She saw something on 'Geraldo' that gave her the idea."

Andie groaned and buried her face in her hands, then looked back up at him with a scowl. "Are you here to try to talk me into moving home and going back to work for Donald, and marrying Steve? Because if you are—"

"Hell, no," Ben said, startled. "I think you'd be crazy to go back there. And I don't know who this Steve guy is, but you can bet your, uh . . . you can bet I don't want you going back to marry him. Haven't you figured that out by now?"

Color crept into her cheeks, but her expression remained stubborn. "You aren't going to try to make me go home?"

"Andie, I'm not going to try to make you do anything. I told the whole bunch of them from the beginning that you're an adult and you have a right to make your own decisions. All I promised to do was find you, make sure you're okay and tell you that your family is worried about you. I did that. Now it's up to you what you want to do next."

Her shoulders relaxed. "I still don't understand why it was necessary for you to lie about writing a travel article."

"I told you," he said patiently. "Your family thought it was a good idea. They made me swear I wouldn't tell you who I was. I let myself be talked into it against my better judgment."

She nodded fatalistically. "They can be like that sometimes."

"No offense, Andie, but your family's even nuttier than my mother. And, trust me, that's saying something!"

She smiled. "I know. They're . . . a bit different."

Ben snorted at the understatement and Andie's smile deepened. "I love them, anyway, of course," she hastily assured him. "Very much. But . . . I needed to get away from them for a while. I needed to find a life for myself."

"I can understand that." He finished his salad and pushed the plate away, wondering how much longer it would be before his entrée arrived. "So how *did* you end up here, anyway? Had you ever heard of this park before?"

Two-thirds of Andie's salad still lay on her plate. She took a tiny bite, washed it down with a sip of iced tea, then shook her head. "No. Actually I'd decided to move to Dallas. I'd visited Texas a few times and always liked it here. Dallas seemed like a good place to find work in a dental office and start a new life."

"So how did you end up as a clown and a magician's assistant?" Ben asked, genuinely puzzled.

Andie laughed softly. "Completely by accident. I was looking through the want ads my first day in Dallas, and I saw an announcement that there were job openings at the theme park. I don't know why, but I decided to visit the place, look around—just out of curiosity. I loved it. I told Mr. Parker that I'd always been good with children, convinced him I would make a great clown, and he gave me a chance to prove it. I fell into helping Milo when his previous assistant left to get married. I spent a couple of weeks learning the act, and we rehearse nearly every morning now before the park opens. It's a lot of fun."

Ben studied her smile. "I get the feeling you haven't had a lot of fun in your life."

She gently shook her head and dark waves of hair swayed softly against the shoulders of her filmy white blouse. "I've had fun. I've had a good life, Ben. I just needed more."

He was beginning to need more himself. More of her kisses, her touches . . .

The striped-shirted waitress appeared suddenly at the table. "Here's your lunch," she announced as she plopped an order of broccoli quiche before Andie. "Let's see, you had the steak and fries, right?" she asked, sliding a plate in front of Ben. "Can I get you anything else?" she asked cheerfully before she left.

Ben turned his attention to his lunch, telling himself to be patient. He'd made progress; Andie didn't seem to be angry with him now. He still wanted to talk to her about her housemate and the bizarre story she'd told him, but that could wait. For now he wanted to concentrate on Andie.

"Are you finished with your shopping?" he asked when they left the restaurant, his hunger—for food, at least—temporarily sated. "Is there something else you need?"

She shook her head. "I bought a couple of paperbacks earlier. I didn't need anything else in particular."

"What were you planning to do next?"

She shrugged. "Go back home."

"I'll follow you."

She gave him a searching look. "Why?"

"I thought we could talk some more," he said, trying to keep his voice casual.

"What about?"

Her suspicion was beginning to frustrate him. "Just talk. Get to know each other better. Spend time together. The usual things men and women do when they're attracted to each other."

Andie looked down at her book bag. Her hair falling forward hid her face from him. "Is that what we are?"

He slipped a hand beneath her chin and lifted her face to his. Ignoring their public surroundings, he kissed her lingeringly. To his satisfaction she didn't resist. "Yes," he said when he released her mouth. "That's what we are."

Her color heightened, Andie cleared her throat and looked away. "You can follow me home," she murmured. "We'll talk."

They'd do a lot more than talk if Ben had his way. He put a hand at her waist as they left the mall, reluctant to be separated from her again now that he'd finally found her.

IT WAS JUST AFTER TWO when Andie unlocked the door to her house and motioned for Ben to follow her inside. She was intensely aware of his nearness, as well as the fact that they were really alone together for the first time. The tiny light flashing on the inexpensive answering machine she and Rosalyn had purchased was a welcome distraction. There was only one message. She pushed the play button.

"Andie, dear," Rosalyn's pleasant voice said clearly, "I just wanted you to know that I'll probably be quite late getting in tonight. Milo and I are going to a movie and then to dinner."

Andie's emotions upon hearing that news were definitely mixed. She was delighted that Milo and Rosalyn were going out again, but now Ben knew that they had several hours alone in the house . . .

Rosalyn's next words made both of them start with surprise. "Hello, Ben," the recording trilled cheerily. "I'm glad you found Andie. I'm sure you'll see she won't be lonely this evening. Have fun, you two."

Andie punched the stop button. It was too late of course. Ben had already heard Rosalyn's mischievous teasing.

"How in the world did she know I..." Ben began, but then stopped and shook his head firmly. "She couldn't have known. She's just damn good at guessing."

Andie didn't bother to argue with him. He'd have to acknowledge the truth about Rosalyn eventually, but he'd get to it in his own way.

So what was she to do with him now? Suddenly the silence seemed nerve-racking. "Would you like some coffee or iced tea?" she said quickly, her voice sounding too loud. "It'll just take me a few minutes to make something. And we have some cookies, I think, maybe part of a cake. Or—"

"No, thank you," Ben cut in quietly, moving a step closer to her.

She gripped her hands in front of her and noted almost absently that the knuckles were turning white. "Are you sure? We have some fruit juice in the refrigerator, if you'd prefer. Or—"

"Andie." Ben slipped a hand beneath her hair to cup her warm cheek. "Are you afraid of me?"

"No," she whispered. "But you make me...nervous."

His firm mouth twitched with a slight smile. "Good nervous or bad nervous?" he asked.

"I'm not sure," she answered honestly.

He lifted his other hand to frame her flushed face between his palms. "Why don't we find out," he murmured. And then he kissed her.

Andie sighed her surrender and slid her arms around his neck, knowing that this had been inevitable, admitting she hadn't really wanted to stop it. If only she could trust herself to enjoy him without becoming too deeply involved, without giving up too much of herself to try to please him, as she'd always done with her family. If only she could trust herself not to fall in love with him.

Ben gathered her closer and pressed her full-length against him for the first time. It was instantly clear to Andie that she wasn't the only one who wanted this intimacy.

He kissed her deeply, thoroughly, again and again, until both of them were gasping for breath. Then he dragged his lips across her cheek to her ear and down to her throat, tasting, nibbling, making shivers of pleasure course through her. His hands were as busy as his mouth, exploring, shaping, caressing, until she was arching eagerly against him, starving for more.

"Andie." His voice was hoarse in her ear, his breath hot against her skin. "If you want me to stop, tell me now."

She caught her breath, knowing exactly what he wanted her to do. What *she* wanted to do.

She lifted her gaze to his face and saw the hunger reflected in his glittering green eyes. But she also saw that he would stop if she asked, that he wouldn't press her for more than she wanted to give. The choice was hers. Play it safe—as she had done all her life—or give in, for once, to reckless impulsive pleasure.

It had never been a difficult decision for her before. She'd always been so cautious, so sensible. She could count the number of times she'd been intimate with a man on the fingers of one hand, and still have a thumb left over. Sex just hadn't been particularly hard to resist before.

But Ben was very different from the other men she'd known, and she was no longer the shy repressed young woman she'd been in Seattle. This time she didn't even want to resist.

She went up on tiptoe to lock her arms more securely around his neck. She strained against him, her breasts flattened against his solid chest, her legs tangled with his. "Don't stop," she whispered. "Please . . . don't stop."

He groaned. "Are you sure? Andie, I—"

She pressed her mouth to his, effectively silencing him. And then she drew back only far enough to meet his eyes. "I know what I want, Ben," she said firmly, pleased with the steadiness of her voice. "I want you."

His eyes flared hotly. "And I want you," he murmured. "I have from the first time I saw you. And you were wearing your clown suit then," he added with a smile that made her knees melt.

She ran an unsteady fingertip across his sexy lower lip. "I guess I could go put on my clown makeup and red nose if that turns you on."

He chuckled. "*You* turn me on," he said. "Just the way you are."

She took a deep breath for courage, slid her hand down to take his and stepped back. "Would you like to see the rest of my house? My bedroom, maybe?"

His fingers closed around hers so tightly she had to suppress a wince. "Yes," he said, his voice husky. "I'd like that very much."

Trying not to let her tension show, Andie led Ben down the short hallway that opened off the tiny living room. Rosalyn's bedroom door was closed, but Andie's stood open. She had to take another deep breath before she stepped through.

"Andie," Ben said gently, "are you sure you want to do this?"

Obviously she hadn't been as successful as she'd hoped at hiding her attack of nerves. "I'm sure," she said, turning toward him with a shaky smile. "I'm just . . . this isn't something I take casually, Ben, despite the short time we've known each other."

"I'm glad," he murmured, touching her cheek. "It isn't casual for me, either. And I feel like I've known you much longer than a few days. I think I've been looking for you for a very long time."

But that was more than Andie was ready to hear just yet. Knowing just how to distract him, she kicked off her sandals and reached for the top button of her blouse.

Ben's hands covered hers. "Let me," he said.

She was wearing a cotton top, pleated shorts, bra and panties. She could have been completely undressed in less than a minute. Ben, however, took his time, stop-

ping to explore the soft skin revealed with the removal
of each garment. He moved his hands and mouth skillfully over every inch of her body—so skillfully she was
shuddering helplessly by the time the last scrap of fab-
ric fell to the floor.

And then he began again.

Needing to touch him, to know his body as intimately as he was learning hers, Andie tore at his
clothes. She quickly had him out of his knit shirt and
shorts. Shyness returned when her fingers touched the
band of his briefs, but Ben covered her hands with his
and urged her to finish the task. He kicked the briefs
away when they fell to his ankles.

Andie caught her breath at the raw male power revealed by his nudity. Then forgot how to breathe al-
together when he pulled her into his arms, bringing
them naked together for the first time.

He was warm and solid and virile. Her aching breasts
flattened against his strong hair-roughened chest, and
she could feel the hardness of him against her flat
stomach. She shivered. "Ben," she whispered.

He kissed her hungrily and she reveled in his impatience, relieved that she wasn't the only one who was
finding it difficult to retain control of her emotions. She
undulated slowly against him, eager to see what would
happen when his control cracked just a bit more.

His reaction left her dazed and breathless. Almost
before she knew it, she was flat on her back on the bed,
her body pinned beneath his larger stronger one, her
mouth crushed beneath his. When he finally lifted his

head to gasp for air, she laughed softly, jubilantly, and tangled her legs with his. He seemed to want her more badly than anyone ever had before, and she responded wholeheartedly to his desire.

"Andie," Ben groaned, his hands clenching at her hips. He moved against her, testingly, probing the damp throbbing entrance to her body. She strained upward, aching for completion.

He held himself rigidly, his body glistening with perspiration, his muscles trembling from the control he exerted. "Wait," he said, his eyes feverish, his cheeks deeply flushed. "I haven't . . . I'm not—"

She covered his mouth with the fingers of one hand. "It's okay," she murmured. "I'm protected. And you needn't worry about your health. I've always been very careful."

"So have I," he murmured, kissing her quickly. "You're safe with me, Andie. Always."

She buried her fingers in his soft dark hair and smiled up at him. Her legs tightened around his hips. "Make love with me, Ben," she whispered.

He murmured something unintelligible and surged forward, claiming her body with his own.

Andie gasped at the power of his possession. Ben paused a moment to allow her to adjust to him, then stirred again when she lifted her hips to encourage him.

Eyes closed, Andie clung to him and felt the muscles bunch beneath his slick skin as he swept her into a rhythmic dance of passion. She moved easily with him, so easily that she could almost believe they'd been made to fit together, that they'd been lovers forever. And then he moved faster and harder. Her body tightened around him and her head tossed restlessly against the pillow. She'd never felt like this, didn't know how to respond to the sensations building ever higher within her.

"Let it go, love," Ben murmured, sliding one hand between them. "Don't hold back now."

His fingers touched her oversensitized skin and she arched mindlessly beneath him. A broken cry left her lips as the final vestiges of reality vanished in an explosion of sensation. She was only dimly aware of Ben's hoarse groan, of the way he went rigid in her arms.

It was a very long time before she could speak, or even think clearly again.

BEN LAY ON HIS BACK, Andie snuggled into his shoulder, his fingers buried in the thick waves of her dark hair. He was finally breathing normally again, and his heart rate had slowed to a semblance of its usual pace. Other than that, everything had changed. He'd made love with Andie McBride, and he would never be entirely the same again.

He kissed the top of her head. "You okay?"

She stirred lazily. "Mm." He could hear the smile in her voice. "Wonderful."

"No regrets?"

"No regrets."

"Good." He smoothed her hair back and kissed her forehead. "Neither do I."

Andie crossed her hands on his chest and propped her chin on top of them. "Tell me about yourself."

He lifted an eyebrow at the unexpected comment. "Like what?"

She shrugged, the movement rubbing her bare skin against his, almost distracting him from the conversation. "Anything. You know so much about me, yet I know very little about you. Nothing that was true, anyway."

He flinched at the mild dig. "I only lied to you about my job," he protested.

"And your name."

"Not even that, really. My name is Benjamin Sherman Luck."

"B.S. Luck," she murmured, her mouth curving into a grin. "Seems appropriate."

"I've heard that before," he said dryly.

"That doesn't surprise me. So . . . ?"

He tried to think of something she might want to know about him. "I grew up in Seattle. I have an older brother, Jon, and a younger sister, Kristin. Jon's married and expecting his first child. Kris is an art teacher in—"

Andie cut in with an exasperated shake of her head. "I know all that. Your mother is a friend of my mother's, remember?"

"Oh. What do you want to know, then?"

"Tell me about your life in Portland. How long have you lived there? How did you get into insurance-fraud investigation? How long have you been doing it? Are you involved with a woman there?" She added the last question a bit too casually.

Ben chuckled. "If there was someone else, would I be here with you now?"

"I don't know."

"Well, I wouldn't," he informed her loftily, echoing her earlier words to him. "I don't operate that way."

"Good."

"I moved to Portland right out of college. Went to work for an insurance agency there. I sort of drifted into fraud investigation because it looked like an interesting line of work. Went free-lance about three years ago, and I've done pretty well with it since. I like being my own boss, setting my own hours, taking time off between assignments if I choose. Like now." The *Reader's Digest* condensed version of his life story, Ben thought with a rueful smile. Had he left out anything important?

"What do you do for fun? When you aren't working?"

"I like sports. Softball, tennis, golf. I do some climbing and some kayaking. I like being outdoors."

"I can tell you stay active," she murmured, running a hand over his left bicep. "You're in very good shape."

He moved a hand down to lingeringly shape her firm bottom. "So are you. Aerobics?"

"Yes. And walking. I like to be outdoors, too."

"Something else we have in common," he said, pleased.

"Yes." Her own smile didn't quite reach her eyes. "When are you going back to Portland?"

He grew serious, as well. "Tired of me already?"

"No. I just want to know what to expect."

"I don't know when I'm going back," he said, watching to see how she'd react to his words. "I'd planned to take a couple of weeks off work. I'd like to spend them here—with you."

Andie moistened her slightly kiss-swollen lips, her eyes shuttered behind her long lashes. "I can't take any time away from work," she warned him. "Tuesdays are my only days off."

"I know. I'll find something else to do while you work. I'll be content to see you when you have time."

She bit her lower lip.

He resisted the urge to soothe those teeth marks with his tongue. "Andie?" he asked, instead. "Do you *want* me to leave?"

"No," she whispered, and he wondered at the hint of sadness in her voice. "I don't want you to go."

"Then I'll stay." *And maybe when I do leave, I'll take you with me, Andie McBride.*

He kept that thought to himself, knowing she wasn't yet ready to consider that possibility.

She shifted her weight again, and her nipples brushed against him. Ben felt his own tighten in response. Andie was beautifully shaped, soft and slight, her breasts small but perfectly rounded. He remembered how nicely they had fit his palms—and his mouth.

Her waist was tiny, her slender hips softly flared. Her legs were long for her height and firm from walking. They had wrapped snugly around his hips.

Meeting his gaze, Andie raised an eyebrow and rubbed her abdomen lightly against his, letting him know she was aware of his suddenly renewed hunger. "I take it you've recovered?" she asked.

He caught her hips and moved her against him. "You noticed."

"It would be hard not to notice."

He grinned. "Oh, it's hard all right."

She sighed loudly and shook her head, but her arms were already winding around his neck. "You really do have strong appetites, don't you?"

"Mm." He nipped at her chin and fitted her more snugly against him. "I don't think I could ever get enough of you."

She closed her eyes and arched her neck to give him access to her throat. "Good," she whispered. She sighed again when his hands moved over her. "Very good," she moaned, and then pressed her mouth to his.

LATE-AFTERNOON SHADOWS were deepening in the corners of the bedroom when Ben stretched and nudged Andie, who lay bonelessly beside him trying to regain enough strength to move her limbs. "Andie?"

"Mmph?"

"I'm hungry."

She giggled. "Speaking of your appetite . . ."

"You could always offer me something other than food," he suggested with a teasing leer.

She pushed her disheveled hair away from her face and sat up. "I think I'd better offer you a sandwich, instead. I'd hate for you to collapse for lack of fuel."

"You're underestimating me," he said, reaching for her.

She evaded his touch and slipped from beneath the tangled sheets to snatch the short robe that lay over the back of a small rocking chair in one corner of the room. Tying it securely around her, she turned back to the bed, where Ben still sprawled, looking disconcertingly big and masculine against her white eyelet-edged sheets. "Ham and Swiss okay with you? I'm not sure I have much more to offer."

"That sounds great," he assured her, sitting up and reaching for his clothes. "I'll help you put something together."

He was right behind her when she stepped out of the bedroom.

Andie paused in front of Rosalyn's door. "Wonder why she left her door closed?" she mused aloud. "She knows how hot it gets in there when the air can't circulate."

Shaking her head at her housemate's absentmindedness, Andie pushed the door open and had turned toward the kitchen before her glimpse into the room registered that something was wrong.

She paused, looked back over her shoulder into Rosalyn's room, then whirled with a gasp. "Oh, my God! *What happened in here?*"

# 9

STARTLED BY ANDIE'S CRY, Ben looked over her shoulder, then moved her aside so he could enter. The room was a shambles—bedclothes wildly tossed, clothing strewn and ripped, pictures pulled off walls, dresser contents broken and scattered. Dusting powder had been thrown over the mess, and the air reeked of the perfume that had once been contained in delicate glass atomizers. One black shoe lay on the otherwise empty dresser top, and colorful costume jewelry sparkled from among the wreckage on the floor.

Ben uttered a short pithy curse. "I don't suppose your housemate is normally so untidy."

"No," Andie whispered, her expression stricken. "Rosalyn is always immaculate."

"That's what I was afraid of." He stepped gingerly over the wreckage and looked around. "Do you see anything missing?"

"It's hard to tell in this mess, but no, I don't." Andie reached down to pick up a glittering necklace. "These are real diamonds. And that's a real pearl bracelet. They're both rather valuable."

Ben had been concentrating almost solely on Andie ever since they'd arrived at the house, but even so, something like this in the living room or kitchen would have been hard to miss. Still . . . he thought they'd better check.

Ten minutes later they'd ascertained that the intruder had gotten in through a window in the kitchen. Andie admitted sheepishly that she'd known the lock was broken on that particular window. Though he was tempted to lecture, Ben bit his tongue and continued the search. Nothing else in the little house had been disturbed. Only Rosalyn's room.

"It's him," Andie murmured through colorless lips. "He's found her again."

"We don't know who did this," Ben reminded her firmly. "It could be anyone."

"Anyone?" she repeated incredulously. "To do something like this? To touch nothing but Rosalyn's possessions? You wouldn't say this is a very clear message?"

It was of course. Ben just hated to admit it. He sighed. "Call the police and then get dressed. An officer will probably come by to file a report—not that there's anything they'll be able to do without some clue as to who did this."

Andie remained where she was, her attention focused inward, her face still pale and stunned. "She'll have to move again. She'll be all alone, in a new city, a new job. I can't let her be alone again, Ben. I'll have to go with her."

"You're not going anywhere," Ben snapped, his stomach clenching at the very possibility. "And neither is Rosalyn—not yet, anyway. Now call the police and get some clothes on, Andie. We have to see what we can do about this mess."

His curt tone got through to her. She glared at him but moved toward the telephone.

Ben ran a weary hand through his hair. He might as well make some coffee, he thought, turning toward the kitchen. They were probably going to need it.

THE SYMPATHETIC but unencouraging police officers had been gone for an hour when Ben and Andie heard the sound of a car in the driveway. Andie was unnaturally subdued, to Ben's concern. "That will be Rosalyn," she said—one of the few sentences she'd spoken since the police had left.

It hadn't helped that the officers had listened politely to Andie's tale of an obsessed rapist/killer, taken a perfunctory look at Rosalyn's room and frankly informed her that there was very little they could do without more information.

"Try to stay calm when you tell her," Ben said.

Andie gave him an annoyed look. "I wasn't planning on having hysterics."

He frowned. "And there's no need to tell her about...well, you know." He figured he and Andie had a right to some privacy in this all-too-public budding relationship.

Her gaze flicked toward the bedroom, then back to his face. "About us, you mean?"

"Yeah."

She shrugged. "I won't have to tell her. She'll know."

"Dammit, Andie, don't start that again. She isn't—"

The front door opened and Rosalyn swept in, her flowing jewel-toned dress swirling around her. "Quarreling again, children?" she began with a smile. And then she stopped, her eyes locked on Andie's face. "What's wrong?"

Ben opened his mouth to speak, but Rosalyn was already headed toward her room, Andie at her heels.

Growling his frustration with the entire affair, Ben followed.

Rosalyn stood very still in her doorway, studying the remains of her belongings with little expression on her softly lined face. Finally she reached out a hand that wasn't quite steady and touched one of the torn garments draped over a small rocker, which matched the one in Andie's room. A spasm of what might have been pain crossed her face and she dropped her hand.

"He was here, wasn't he?" Andie asked in a strained whisper.

Rosalyn nodded. "He was here."

Andie put an arm around her housemate's fragile shoulders. "He must have thought you'd be here. When you weren't, he—"

"No," Rosalyn interrupted. "He knew I wasn't here. This is a message. He's toying with me. He isn't quite ready to strike. The . . . the numbers are wrong. The date, I believe. He's waiting for a particular date and possibly a special time. I can't pick up anything more specific."

"Dammit, if you know all that, why can't you just give us a name?" Ben demanded impatiently. "Tell us where he is now, so we can have him arrested and put away."

"I wish I could," Rosalyn said, not the least bit upset by his outburst. "But I can't. It just doesn't work that way."

"Then what good is this gift of yours?" he asked, still furious at the thought that someone had been in Andie's house, that she might have been here when he'd broken in. A man who'd raped, and who'd killed, if Rosalyn was to be believed, and it was beginning to appear that she had been telling the truth—at least about someone being after her. "Seems to me that it's gotten you into a hell of a lot of trouble, but it's not doing much to get you out of it."

"Ben!" Andie protested. The spark of temper in her dark eyes gave him a small measure of satisfaction. He'd rather see her angry than wounded and vulnerable.

"It's all right, Andie," Rosalyn said with a faint smile. "Ben is right, of course. My gift has been difficult to live with at times. It's not something I ever asked for, Ben. In fact . . ."

Her voice trailed away, and her eyes were filled suddenly with such sadness that even Ben was shaken. She turned away before he could say anything, her manner brisk again. "I'll have to get this mess cleared away," she said, "and then I'll start packing. I have to get away from here."

"I'll pack, too," Andie said. "I'm going with you, Rosalyn."

"Oh, Andie, dear, of course you aren't going with me. You have your own life to live. I refuse to let you get any more entangled in my troubles. I'll find a way to contact you occasionally. I promise."

"I'm going with you," Andie said again, her voice firm, her chin stubbornly set. "I won't let you be alone anymore."

"Dammit, would you both just be quiet!" Ben said explosively, his voice booming in the small demolished room.

Startled, Andie and Rosalyn turned to stare at him.

Satisfied he had their attention, Ben lowered his voice to a more normal level. "Neither of you is going anywhere, is that clear? If I have to tie you to your beds, neither of you is stepping foot out of this house tonight."

"You have—"

"Ben, dear—"

He cut them both off with a slashing movement of one hand. "I'm staying here tonight, and every night until we either catch this guy or find you both someplace safer to stay. I've got some contacts in the law-enforcement community. I'll start calling them tomorrow, and we'll make more plans then. In the meantime, we're all tired and tense. As soon as this mess is cleaned up, we'll try to get some rest. I'll, uh, sleep on the couch in the living room."

"Don't feel as though you have to observe the proprieties for my sake, Benjamin," Rosalyn murmured. Her expression made him suspect she knew where he had spent most of the afternoon. "The couch really isn't very comfortable."

Ben felt his cheeks warm with a flush, and he turned away from her all-too-perceptive eyes. "What can I do to help in here?" he asked gruffly.

Ben and Andie hadn't had a chance to eat anything since early afternoon. As soon as Rosalyn's room had been restored to some semblance of order—though most of her possessions had been damaged beyond repair—Andie insisted on making Ben a thick sandwich. He refused to eat unless she joined him. She only picked at her food, but finally ate enough to satisfy him.

Although she'd already had dinner with Milo, Rosalyn sat with them as they ate. She made a fresh pot of coffee and sipped at hers with a distracted air. There was little conversation during the meal.

Ben was the one who finally broke the thoughtful silence. "How long have you been doing this?" he asked Rosalyn. "This psychic thing, I mean."

Andie looked up, immediately defensive on her friend's behalf.

Rosalyn lifted a hand to calm Andie. "He's only asking a question, dear. Don't start a quarrel now." And then she turned to Ben, her expression unruffled. "Twenty-five years ago, my husband, our eight-year-old daughter and I were in a terrible car accident. My husband and daughter were killed. I was in a coma for several days and was not expected to survive."

Ben squirmed in his chair, wishing that he'd kept his mouth shut. "I'm sorry. I didn't—"

"After I awoke, I soon discovered I wasn't quite the same person I'd been before the accident," Rosalyn continued quietly. "I began to have . . . visions. Premonitions about other people—even total strangers— that were uncannily accurate. I was given a battery of tests by a local researcher, who concluded I had some special abilities." She sighed deeply. "Now perhaps you can understand what I meant when I said that I didn't ask for my gift. In acquiring it, I lost my family."

Ben still could not believe in her psychic ability, but there was no denying the quiet suffering in her eyes. Fascinated despite his ingrained skepticism, he asked, "So then you started telling fortunes?"

Rosalyn answered patiently. "No. Not at first. I had never worked outside the home, and I had few marketable skills. And my gift tended to make some people nervous, as I'm sure you understand," she said with an indulgent smile. "My financial situation, especially with my medical bills, grew rather desperate. A friend suggested I start charging for consultations. It wasn't something I particularly wanted to do, but eventually I had no other choice. I opened a small consulting business, and it became quite successful. And then a broad-minded police detective asked my advice on a couple of his cases, with promising results. I worked

with him several times over a five-year period, with
perhaps an eighty percent success rate . . ."

Ben's eyebrows rose at the impressive figure.

"And then, two years ago, he persuaded a detective
from another precinct to bring me in on the serial-rape
case. The other detective had little faith in my abilities,
but his case was going nowhere, and he was getting
desperate. I've already told you what happened next."

"You sensed some facts about the rapist that were
leaked to the newspaper. The facts were apparently accurate enough to make the guy nervous. He came after
you and hasn't given up in two years, even though
you've moved several times to elude him."

"Yes." She nodded in satisfaction at his concise sum-
mation of the tale she'd told him that morning, and then
her eyes clouded. "I'm not sure how he continues to find
me, but he seems to enjoy toying with me. He thrives
on the sense of power he gets from striking fear in others."

"Typical of a rapist."

Rosalyn nodded. "Apparently."

"Do you know when he'll make his next move?"

Her mouth tightened. "No."

Ben nodded curtly. "I don't want either of you to be
alone from now on, is that clear? No coming home to
an empty house, either of you. Either come together or
with me."

"We should tell Milo," Andie said. "He'll make himself available for Rosalyn."

"I really didn't want to worry him with this," Rosalyn murmured, looking distressed.

Ben didn't know how much protection the little magician could provide, but he figured it wouldn't hurt to have at least one more person they could trust watching out for anything unusual. At least he didn't suspect Milo of being a homicidal rapist, he thought wryly. "Andie's right that Milo should be told," he said. "It isn't fair to keep him in the dark, Rosalyn. He should be warned about the potential of danger."

"I've endangered him . . . and Andie . . . and perhaps even you," Rosalyn whispered, looking down at her lap. "Just by being with me, you are in peril. It's all because of me."

"Rosalyn—" Andie began.

Ben spoke over her impulsive reassurances. "You can't keep running, Rosalyn. And you can't avoid making friends or becoming involved with others because of this man. Something has to be done to stop him."

"Like what?" Andie demanded.

Rosalyn, too, was looking at Ben, and both women seemed to expect him to suggest some solution to their predicament. Ben, of course, had no suggestion to make, at least not yet. This was Jon's line of business, not his, he reasoned grimly. "I'm going to make some phone calls," he said. "I suggest the two of you get some sleep."

Rosalyn didn't linger. Her steps were weary when she left the kitchen after bidding them good-night.

Andie stayed behind. "Who are you going to call?"

"My brother, for one."

"The homicide detective in Seattle?"

"Yeah. Maybe he can give me some idea of what we should do next."

"It's kind of late to call him, isn't it?"

Ben glanced at his watch. It was nearly eleven. "It's not even nine in Seattle," he reminded her.

"Oh. Do you mind if I stay with you when you call?"

"No, of course not." Ben suddenly realized that he hadn't even kissed her since they'd left her bedroom almost five hours earlier. He reached out and pulled her into a hard hug. "You okay?"

Her arms went tightly around his waist. "I think so," she murmured, nestling her head into the crook of his shoulder. "I'm still a bit dazed."

From the break-in or their lovemaking? Ben thought it might be a combination of both. He tilted her face up to his and kissed her lingeringly. And then he reluctantly let her go. "I'd better call Jon."

She nodded and ran the tip of her tongue across her lips as though still tasting his kiss. Ben almost pulled her back into his arms right then. He had to turn away from her to resist.

"I'VE BEEN TRYING to call you all evening," Jon barked as soon as Ben got through to him. "You've got half-a-dozen messages from me at the hotel."

"I haven't gone back there yet. What have you got for me?"

"There was a psychic named Rosalyn Carmody who got involved in a rape/murder case in California. Apparently she gave enough clues that the police came close to catching the guy—and then the rapes stopped and the psychic became his target. She left the area two years ago and hasn't been heard from since by the officers who'd worked with her."

"She's been on the move," Ben explained, leaning against the kitchen counter as he talked. Andie stood close beside him, openly listening to his end of the conversation. "The guy's almost caught up with her a couple of times, but she's managed to evade him."

"Hell. You already knew all this."

"I only learned it today."

"Oh. I still don't have anything on the magician."

"Forget the magician," Ben said. "He's harmless. We have something a lot more serious to worry about."

"Like what?" Jon asked warily.

"The bastard has apparently found Rosalyn again. And no one close to her is safe until he's caught."

"Damn. You're sure about this?"

Ben told his brother about the viciously trashed room. "Nothing else in the house was touched. The message couldn't be clearer."

"Ben," Jon said thoughtfully, "there is one other possibility."

"I'd like to hear it."

"The woman could have trashed the room herself."

Ben was startled by the suggestion—one that had never occurred to him. "Why would she have done that?"

"For attention? To give more credence to her claims about the rapist? Hell, who knows. You're the fraud investigator. You know more about these things than I do."

Ben had to concede that he'd seen fraud take a lot of strange turns. Had he been officially assigned to this case, he probably would have considered Rosalyn's involvement himself.

He'd gotten too personally involved, he thought grimly. With Andie, and maybe with the whole strange lot of them. "I suppose it's possible that she could have trashed the room, herself, but she—"

"No, it is *not* possible!" Andie said with a gasp, grabbing Ben's arm. "How could you even suggest something like that? I thought you believed her now!"

"Andie, it's just a possibility we have to consider," Ben answered reasonably, aware that Jon was hearing every word.

"No," she insisted. "Not even a possibility. Why would she have done such a thing? And, besides, she *couldn't* have done it. I was here when she left this morning. I certainly would have heard anyone making a mess like that, and I didn't."

"She could have come back to the house after you left for the mall."

"I'm sure if you'll check you'll find she was at work all morning. And she was with Milo afterward."

"You can always check her story out," Jon said in Ben's ear.

"I'll check it out," Ben agreed, then added for Andie's sake, "I don't really think it's a probability, but I'll look into it, anyway."

Andie didn't look particularly mollified.

Jon suggested several other leads for Ben to pursue. Ben made a mental note of all of them, trusting his brother's judgment and experience. And then Jon muttered a curse and said, "I wish I could get away to give you a hand. Maybe the two of us together could come up with some way to catch this guy. But—"

"But you can't leave Amanda with the baby due so soon," Ben finished for him. "I wouldn't let you even if you suggested it."

"You keep your guard up, you hear, little brother? This whole situation sounds pretty weird to me."

"You've got that straight," Ben muttered. "But I'll be careful. Oh, and, Jon, if you need to reach me from now on, you can try this number." He read Andie's number aloud from the base of the telephone. "Got that?"

"Yeah. Where is it?"

"Andie's place. I'll be staying here for now keeping an eye on the two women until we decide what to do."

"Keeping an eye on the women," Andie muttered beside him. "Of all the macho condescending . . ."

Ben cleared his throat and bade his brother goodbye, promising to stay in touch.

"I can't believe he suggested Rosalyn trashed her own room," Andie complained when Ben had hung up. "Or that you even acknowledged the possibility. How could you do that?"

"Until I'm certain you're safe I'm going to consider every possibility," Ben said flatly. "If I had my way I'd ship you off to Seattle or Portland without a second thought. But since I know you'd refuse to go—"

"You've got that straight," she muttered, deliberately quoting his words to Jon.

"I'm not letting you out of my sight until we know exactly what's going on here," Ben finished without pausing.

"You can hardly watch me every minute. And besides, it's Rosalyn he's after, not me. Why aren't you more concerned about her safety?"

"I am concerned about her," Ben answered candidly. "I'd hate to see her harmed. But you come first with me, Andie. I'd have thought you'd have figured that out by now."

She flushed and avoided his gaze. "I . . ."

She still wasn't ready for him to tell her exactly how he felt about her. He figured the best way to let her know was just to show her.

She gasped as he swung her into his arms, then steadied herself against his shoulders. Ben crushed her mouth beneath his when she started to protest. By the time the kiss ended, she'd obviously forgotten what she'd started to say.

Ben didn't give her time to remember. Instead, he carried her to her bedroom and kicked the door closed behind them.

## 10

BEN INSISTED on driving Rosalyn and Andie to work the
next morning. Rock music blasted from the radio when
he started the engine, making all three jump. Ben grimaced apologetically and immediately lowered the
volume. "Sorry. I tend to turn it up too loud when I'm
in the car alone."

"That's quite all right, dear," Rosalyn said from the
back seat. "I rather like Whitesnake's music. It's a
shame they broke up, isn't it?"

Ben choked. Andie laughed at his expression. "Don't
try to pigeonhole her," she advised him.

"Tell me about it," he muttered, backing carefully out
of the driveway.

Though he stood well back so as not to interfere with
her work, Ben didn't let Andie out of his sight for more
than a few minutes at a time that day. Several of her coworkers commented teasingly about her newly ac-
quired "shadow," particularly when Ben made it clear
he was no longer working on his travel article. He was
staking his claim, and the others recognized the move.
As did Andie, her frown told him. Still, everyone but
Andie seemed to accept the development readily
enough.

When he wasn't watching Andie, Ben watched the crowds at the park, looking for anyone suspicious among the family groups and day-care outings and packs of teenagers. Remembering Rosalyn's description, he concentrated especially on fair skin and tattoos, neither of which were scarce. Was *everyone* wearing tattoos these days? He blinked in disapproval when a four- or five-year-old kid strutted past sporting a colorful eagle on one scrawny bicep; he was only marginally relieved when he realized the tattoo was of the stick-on variety.

The only unpleasant incident that morning happened just before noon when Andie accidentally jostled a greasy biker in chains and leather, causing the man to spill his beer. The guy, who was obviously quite drunk already, went into a rage, shoved Andie and frightened the group of preschoolers she was entertaining. Ben was just about to take him on when two park security guards rushed up and firmly led the loudly protesting biker away.

"You okay?" Ben asked Andie, who'd backed prudently out of the way to let the security guards deal with the situation.

"I'm fine," she assured him. "I just hate it that the children were distressed."

"Does that sort of thing happen often here?"

She shook her bewigged head. "There are always going to be a few troublemakers, but on the whole we don't have many problems. That guy was just a jerk—

he wasn't even supposed to have the beer out on the midway."

"You're sure you're okay? He pushed you pretty hard."

"Ben, I'm fine. Don't smother me, okay?" Her eyes were serious beneath the whimsical makeup.

He could tell this was important to her. He held up both hands in a gesture of surrender and took a step backward. "All right. I'll let you get back to work."

"I'd appreciate it," she said, then plastered on her broad clown smile and turned toward a group of giggling kids.

Ben and Andie had lunch with Rosalyn and Milo in Milo's tiny mobile home. At Ben's urging, Rosalyn told Milo about the threat she'd been living under for the past two years. Predictably the mild-mannered little man was quite disturbed. "Rosalyn, dear, you should have told me about it before this," he chided her, reaching out to take her hand in his. "Perhaps I could have helped you in some way."

"There's really nothing you could have done, Milo," Rosalyn answered gently. "I didn't want to worry you."

"I am worried," Milo said, his broad forehead crinkled deeply. "You know how deeply I care about you. I can't bear to think of you being harmed."

Rosalyn smiled tremulously and patted Milo's hand. Ben glanced away from them, feeling as though he was spying on something outsiders weren't meant to witness.

Ben no longer considered Milo a threat to Andie—
or to anyone else, for that matter. The man was
friendly, open and obviously harmless. He'd told Ben
he'd once been an accountant but had abandoned his
thriving practice twenty years ago, at the age of forty,
to pursue his lifelong dream of being a magician. He'd
never married and had lived with his invalid mother
until her death. When he'd made the decision to change
his life so drastically, his coworkers had thought he'd
lost his mind. But even though he would never achieve
fame or fortune as a magician, he'd never been happier
than he was now, delighting the children who visited
Big Top.

It soon became obvious that Milo was as firmly convinced of Rosalyn's abilities as Andie claimed to be. Ben
clung to his own skepticism with a touch of despera-
tion, unwilling to concede the existence of forces beyond his control. It was growing increasingly hard to
deny them, though, particularly at those times when
Rosalyn hit him with a zinger about himself that was
just a bit too accurate for comfort.

"You must be excited that your brother and his wife
are expecting their first child, Benjamin," she said as
they brought their luncheon to an end. "I'm sure you'll
enjoy being an uncle."

"Andie told you about that?" Ben asked.

Andie only smiled and shook her head.

"You needn't worry about your sister-in-law," Rosalyn added musingly. "Both she and your niece will be
just fine."

*Niece?* Even Jon and Amanda didn't know the gender of their child. Ben gave Rosalyn a dry look and murmured, "At least you have a fifty-percent chance of being right."

She chuckled, apparently enjoying his stubborn incredulity. "The child will be born this evening, sometime between six and eight. You can tell me then if I'm correct."

"The baby's not due until the end of the month. You can't possibly know that it will be early."

"Congratulations, Ben," Andie said with a bright smile. "By tonight you'll be an uncle."

Ben frowned at all of them and received three indulgent smiles in return.

That afternoon they stopped by Ben's hotel, where he gathered his belongings, retrieved his messages and then checked out. Neither Andie nor Rosalyn commented when he told them what he'd done. Both knew he would not leave them unprotected at night, no matter how loudly they asserted their ability to defend themselves. Their next stop was the supermarket, where Ben insisted on paying for groceries. After all, he pointed out reasonably, he'd be staying with them for at least a few days, and he tended to eat a great deal.

Jon called at ten o'clock, just as Rosalyn, Ben and Andie had finished clearing the kitchen and had settled down to watch the evening news. Katherine Brooke Luck had arrived at 7:30 p.m., Seattle time. Mother and daughter were both doing fine. Jon was exuberant, as was young A.J. Grandmothers Jessie Luck and

Eleanor Hightower were also gleefully celebrating the happy event, along with Grandpa Luck and Kristin, who was delighted to have become an aunt.

"Congratulations," Andie said again when Ben hung up the phone and dazedly made the announcement. She rose to kiss his cheek, then drew back with a mischievous sparkle in her dark eyes. "You still think Rosalyn just makes lucky guesses?"

Ben looked slowly from Andie's teasing smile to Rosalyn's sympathetic expression. "Hell," he muttered, running a hand through his hair. "I don't know what to think anymore."

Rosalyn patted his arm as she walked past him. "Take your time, dear. Now, if the two of you will excuse me, I'm going to bed. See you in the morning."

Though Ben half expected her to do so, Andie didn't tease him any more about his difficulty in dealing with her friend's psychic ability. Instead, she settled into his arms on the couch and gazed absently at the television set, her thoughts obviously far away.

Ben nestled her into his shoulder, perfectly content to be just where he was. He could hold Andie like this for hours without complaint, he decided, resting his cheek against her hair. He allowed his thoughts to drift—from the deep pleasure he felt at thinking of his new niece in Seattle to his concern about the man who might still be waiting for the mysterious right time to kill Rosalyn. He'd talked to the local police by telephone that afternoon. Again his concerns had been met with sympathy but a frustrating lack of reassurance.

There was simply nothing that could be done until the police had more to go on. As vexed as he'd been, Ben had to admit he understood their position.

He just wished there was something more he could do to ensure Andie's safety.

After a long while, Andie sighed and stirred against him. "It's getting late."

He brushed her forehead with a kiss. "I'm ready to go to bed if you are," he said, his pulse picking up a bit in anticipation.

She looked at him, and her expression was sober. "We need to talk about this."

He lifted an eyebrow. "You're *not* ready to go to bed?"

She shook her head at his obtuseness. "I meant we need to talk about your staying here—and how long it's going to last."

"Tired of me already?" He tried to keep the question light, but suspected he wasn't entirely successful.

She bit her lower lip. "No," she said after a moment. "I'm not tired of you."

"Good." He was a long way from being tired of her; in fact, he couldn't imagine that ever happening.

"But you can't just stay here indefinitely," she said, squirming around to look up at him. "Your home, your job, your life are all back in Oregon."

His life was here. Ben stared at her as the realization hit him like a blow between the eyes. From now on, his life was wherever Andie was—Texas, Oregon or anywhere else she might lead him.

It was a daunting admission for a man who'd always valued his freedom, lived his life on his own terms. Except for his immediate family, he'd made no commitments, allowed no ties to bind him since he'd left for college when he was eighteen.

"Ben?" Andie was looking at him oddly. He wondered how many times she'd said his name while he'd struggled to come to grips with this massive change in his life.

"Uh . . . let's not worry about the future right now," he said, shaking off his strange mood. "As you pointed out it's getting late, and you have to work tomorrow."

"But—"

"Andie." He cupped her face in his hands, holding her gaze with his. "I don't know what's going to happen—with us, with this guy who's after Rosalyn, with anything. I only know that, for now, I'm where I want to be. Okay?"

She sighed almost soundlessly and nodded her head between his palms. "Okay. If you're sure."

He kissed her, then released her and said, "Now, what were you saying about going to bed?"

She rose and held out her hand to him. "I'm ready when you are."

He smiled. "That's what I wanted to hear."

BEN LAY AWAKE long after Andie fell asleep in his arms.

He should have known, he mused resignedly, that when he finally fell in love, it wouldn't be a peaceful uncomplicated event. Here he was, head over heels in love with a woman he'd known less than a week, a woman from a family even nuttier than his mother, a woman who worked as a clown and lived with a psychic who was the apparent target of a murderous madman.

He must be a real glutton for punishment.

He didn't doubt that his feelings for Andie were real. No woman had ever made him feel the way she did. No one had ever suited him so well. He tightened his arm around her bare shoulders, noting in satisfaction that she fit perfectly against him. He loved her spirit, her temper, her loyalty, her courage. She was his now, and he'd do whatever it took to convince her of that. And to protect her.

Ben would willingly sacrifice his own life to save Andie's. But he had no intention of letting things get to that extreme. Whatever happened he was ready.

The jerk who'd been toying with Rosalyn didn't know what he'd taken on now that he'd become a threat to Benjamin Luck's woman.

ON THURSDAY Ben realized that he wasn't the only one determined to protect Andie McBride. Problem was, everyone else seemed to be protecting her from *him*.

A large female clown in a garishly flowered dress approached him early that morning while he waited for Andie to emerge from the dressing room. "You're that Ben guy, aren't you?" she asked in a deep resonant voice.

He lifted an eyebrow. "Yes?"

"Andie's a sweet girl. You be nice to her."

The blunt command caused Ben's mouth to twitch with amusement. "I'll do that."

She nodded curtly. "Good." She started to move away, then stopped to look suspiciously over her shoulder. "You're not one of those weirdos who wear women's underwear or anything like that, are you?"

Ben had to swallow hard before he could answer. "No," he said, his voice a bit unsteady. "Just the standard plain white cotton men's briefs."

Again she nodded, apparently satisfied with his answer. "Good. See you around."

As he'd done the day before, Ben stayed close to Andie without interfering with her work. He was munching popcorn and watching a little boy trying to take a first bite out of an enormous candy apple when a hand fell on his shoulder. Ben looked around—and then up. "Oh. Hello, Milton."

The seven-and-a-half-foot thin man nodded with regal dignity. "Sherman, or is it Luck?"

"Luck," Ben admitted, wondering how his real name had made the grapevine so quickly.

"Wasn't very nice of you to lie to Andie about your job. You should have just told her you were working for her family."

"Yes, I know. I've apologized to her."

"We've grown quite fond of Andie here. We wouldn't want to see her upset."

His neck still craned upward, Ben nodded rapidly. "I understand."

Milton pursed his lips, studied Ben through narrowed eyes for a moment longer, then dropped his hand. "Rosalyn trusts you, so you must be okay. Still . . . you watch your step, you hear?"

"You bet."

A curvaceous bleached blonde whom Ben recognized as the circus equestrian approached him at around noon. "I'm Polly," she said. "You're Ben, aren't you?"

"Yes." Though resigned to another lecture about being nice to Andie, Ben tried to forestall it by adding, "I've admired your riding during the circus performances. You're very good with horses."

"Grew up on a ranch," she said matter-of-factly. And then she reached for his left hand. To his bewilderment, she studied it intently.

"Um, are you a psychic, like Rosalyn?" he asked, though his hand wasn't tingling the way it did when Rosalyn held it.

Polly shook her head, and tapped his ring finger with one long red fingernail. "Looking for tan lines," she explained. "You wouldn't happen to have a wife and a houseful of kids back home, would you?"

"No wife and no kids. I've never married."

She released his hand. Her smile was bright but didn't quite reach her eyes. "You'd better be telling the truth. Everyone's seen the way you've been cozying up to Andie."

"Yes. Apparently they have," Ben agreed.

Polly patted his cheek. Her voice oozed with sweetness. "Hurt her, and I'll have Tiny cut you into little pieces and mix you in with the horse feed. Got that?"

Ben choked. "Uh...yeah. You've made yourself quite clear."

Smiling in smug satisfaction, Polly left him with a provocative roll of her hips.

"What was that all about?" Andie demanded, looking a bit miffed as she approached. "Polly was all over you."

"She was just telling me what a nice couple you and I make," Ben replied promptly, squeezing her waist.

She glanced around and quickly moved away. "Behave yourself," she ordered, though she was smiling. "Clowns aren't supposed to carry on in front of innocent children."

"Carry on?" Ben asked with interest. "Is that what we were doing?"

She only shook a gloved finger at him and turned back to her work, leaving him to wonder who would deliver the next dire warning.

It was nice to know Andie had so many good friends, he thought ruefully, but this could become a bit tiresome.

They had lunch in the employee cafeteria. Andie had changed into a loose sleeveless sundress and wore her dark hair brushed softly around her shoulders. Ben couldn't take his eyes off her. It always delighted him to see her transformed so swiftly from absurd clown to stunning young woman.

A sultry raven-haired woman with a blatantly sexy walk and very deep cleavage stopped at their table. "Why don't you introduce me to your friend, Andie?" she murmured. Her husky voice reminded Ben of Kathleen Turner's Jessica Rabbit.

Andie glanced up from her lunch. "Cassie, this is Ben Luck," she said obligingly. "Ben, Cassie is—"

"The animal trainer in the circus," he cut in. "I've admired your performances."

The woman smiled, looking almost as feline as the huge cats she worked with. "Thank you. I enjoy my work. My cats are very sweet, but they can be deadly. Perhaps you'd like to stop by and let me introduce you to them?"

"Maybe I'll do that—sometime," Ben said, knowing he would do no such thing. He wasn't getting anywhere near this woman's "sweet" pets.

"They wouldn't hurt a fly," Cassie assured him. "Unless of course," she purred, "someone hurt me—or one of my friends. But I don't think that's going to happen, do you?"

"No. I'm sure you and your friends are quite safe," Ben replied, speaking almost by rote now.

Cassie nodded and glided away.

Andie squirmed uncomfortably in her seat and cleared her throat. "Uh, sorry about the poorly veiled warning. I don't know what gets into Cassie sometimes."

Ben shrugged. "Actually she was much more subtle about it than the others."

Andie's dark eyes went wide. "The others?"

He nodded. "Polly, Milton, some guy pushing a broom through the park, the lemonade vendor, the teenager in the bear suit. Oh, and a very large lady clown. She seemed particularly concerned about my taste in underwear."

Andie groaned and hid her flushed face in her hands. "Oh, my God. Don't tell me they've all been threatening you."

"In their own interestingly individual ways."

"Oh, Ben, I'm so sorry. I can't believe they did that."

He smiled at her dismay. "It's okay, Andie. They care about you. I think that's nice."

She shook her head. "You don't understand. I don't need a bunch of people looking out for me. I'm perfectly capable of taking care of myself. Why can't anyone accept that?"

"Andie, if they didn't think you could take care of yourself, they'd probably be doing everything they could to keep us apart," he said logically. "They aren't trying to stop me from seeing you. They're only letting me know that they care about you, and they want you to be treated nicely. Is there really anything wrong with that?"

"How can you defend them this way when they're treating you with such suspicion?" she demanded in frustration. "Cassie just threatened to feed you to her cats, for crying out loud!"

"Polly was going to grind me up and feed me to her horses," Ben said musingly. "I'm not sure which is the worse fate actually."

Andie groaned again and ran her hands through her hair. Then she raised her head to see Blake standing beside the table. "This guy bugging you again, Andie?" he asked.

She lowered her hands and pounded the table. "Don't you dare start threatening him. Is that clear?"

Blake lifted an eyebrow in response to her vehemence. "Quite clear." He looked over their plates, idly picked up a boiled egg and an apple from Andie's and a cellophane-wrapped muffin from Ben's. Before either of them could protest, he sent the food into motion, juggling the items with lazy movements that made the action look simple. "Has he talked you into quitting the circus and moving back home to the family yet?" he asked Andie.

"No, he hasn't even tried," Andie replied crossly. "All he wants to do is make sure I'm all right."

"And are you?"

"Of course I am! Why wouldn't I be?"

Ben leaned back in his chair, watching the circling food and waiting for Blake to respond.

Blake shrugged, and Ben wondered how he did that without interrupting his juggling. "There's a rumor going around that Rosalyn's in some sort of trouble. Do you know anything about it?"

"Where did you hear this rumor?" Ben asked before Andie could speak.

Blake glanced Ben's way, and Ben noted—not for the first time—the intensity of that icy blue gaze. Blake's casual indolence was deceptive, he decided. There was more to this man than he allowed anyone to see. The question was, what was Blake hiding? And how, if at all, did it concern Rosalyn or Andie?

Ben made a promise to himself never to let Andie out of his sight when Blake was anywhere near.

Andie looked from Blake to Ben and then back again. "Why don't you stop playing with our lunch and run along now, Blake? I'm sure you have better things to do."

Blake gave her a cocky grin, set the egg and the apple back on her plate and turned toward the door. "See you later, Andie."

"Hey!" Ben protested. "The muffin."

"My favorite kind," Blake replied without looking around. "Thanks, Luck. Maybe I'll buy you one sometime."

"That son of a—"

Andie cut in quickly. "You and Blake seem to bring out the worst in each other."

"I guess you could say that." Ben was still glaring after the other man. He'd wanted that muffin. And it had been the last one, dammit.

"Why do you dislike him so much?"

He swiveled back and frowned at Andie's puzzled face. "Because of the way he looks at you," he said bluntly.

"How is that?"

"Like he wouldn't mind dipping you in chocolate and having you for dessert."

She blinked, then blushed. "Honestly, Ben."

"Yes, honestly," he mocked her. "And if he keeps looking at you that way, I may just have to rearrange his teeth."

"There's nothing worse than a couple of boys in men's bodies displaying their machismo," Andie complained.

Ben stabbed his fork into a spear of overcooked broccoli and pointedly ignored her.

When they finished lunch it was almost time for Andie to start dressing for the circus performance. Ben gathered his plate and utensils. "Do you have any errands to run this afternoon, or were you planning to go straight home?"

"No, I don't have any plans. Why?"

"No reason. I thought I'd cook my world-famous chicken casserole for dinner tonight. You and Rosalyn are in for a culinary treat."

She cocked an eyebrow. "World famous?"

He nodded solemnly. "Trust me. Once you've tasted my chicken casserole, you'll never—"

A startled cry cut off his words. "Fire!" a woman called from the doorway of the cafeteria. "The fortune-teller's tent!"

Andie dropped her tray, oblivious to the clatter of plastic dinnerware. "Oh, my God!"

Ben set his own tray on the table and took Andie's forearm in a steadying grasp. "Let's go," he said. He tried to keep his voice calm, but he was as concerned as Andie.

The chances were slim that this fire was an accident.

# 11

A CROWD HAD GATHERED at the scene, impeding the efforts of park employees trying to control the fire until emergency equipment arrived from the Mercury Fire Department. Tiny, serving as a one-man crowd-control crew, held spectators back with massive outspread arms. Far off to one side, a tall graying man in an immaculate suit looked on, his expression clearly annoyed. Ben recognized him as Mr. Parker, the demanding owner of the park.

Ben and Andie pushed through the gawkers, intent on getting to Rosalyn. They passed Pam, the young receptionist, who was trying to get away from the chaos. "Rosalyn's okay," she assured them, seeing the concern on their faces. "She smelled smoke and got everyone out of the tent before the flames spread."

"Thank God," Andie murmured. Still holding her arm, Ben silently echoed the sentiment. During the past few days, he'd become quite fond of the eccentric psychic.

Rosalyn was standing well out of danger, staring at the burning fabric-covered structure while Milo hovered around her. Andie took her hand. Ben stood in front of her and searched her expressionless face. "Rosalyn?" he asked gently. "Are you all right?"

Her eyes were haunted when they met his. "He's here," she whispered. "In the park. Now."

Ben stiffened. "Where?"

She shook her head. "I don't know."

"In this crowd? Is he watching now?"

"I don't know. I..." She moistened her lips. "Maybe."

"Damn." After a quick glance at Andie's tightly drawn expression, Ben turned to study the crowd. So many curious faces, so many strangers. Plenty of unsavory-looking characters among the respectably attired family types, but who was to say the guy didn't look like an ordinary accountant or stockbroker? Rosalyn's description had been so vague.

He looked from a button-down preppy with a permanently bored expression to an unkempt man holding a beer and grinning at the excitement. Could it be either of them? Was the shaggy one the guy who'd pushed Andie the day before?

A man in a battered cowboy hat, a sleeveless T-shirt, dusty jeans and worn boots bumped against Ben while trying to get a better look at the fire. "Sorry," he muttered, and moved on—but not before Ben caught a glimpse of the tattoo on the man's arm. *Was he the one?*

"Damn," Ben growled again, thoroughly frustrated. What the hell was he doing, anyway? There was still nothing more to go on than Rosalyn's mysterious feelings. As eerily accurate as she'd been thus far, Ben still wasn't prepared to fully accept her gift. He was a trained investigator. He put his trust in facts, not feelings.

Sirens blared over the noise of the crowd, and uniformed security guards sent the spectators on their way, politely encouraging them to return to their entertainment and let the fire fighters do their jobs. The two-by-four-and-fabric structure was almost gone now; there was little left to do but prevent the fire from spreading to other park structures. Ben didn't think that was a danger. The fortune-teller's tent had been separate from the other attractions, and there was no wind to spread the flames.

Ben fully intended to look over the scene as soon as the fire fighters had finished their work. He'd investigated enough suspicious fires to know what to look for to determine where and how this one had started.

Blake walked over to where Ben stood with Andie, Rosalyn and Milo. His face was smudged with soot and he was buttoning one long sleeve of his now-grubby yellow shirt. "Everyone okay here?"

"Yes, we're fine. What happened to you?" Andie asked, studying his uncharacteristically disheveled appearance.

"I was just making sure everyone got out safely," he replied with a shrug. "I think I'll go clean up."

"You just happened to be around when the fire started?" Ben asked. Seemed like Blake was always around when things went wrong, he realized with a sudden frown. Or was his personal antagonism toward Blake getting in the way of his objectivity?

"That's right," Blake agreed evenly. His expression dared Ben to make any more of it.

Ben let it go. After all, he had nothing more than a feeling to base his suspicions on, and hadn't he just reminded himself that a feeling wasn't enough?

Rosalyn gasped and glanced at her watch. "Milo, Andie, it's time for you to get ready for the circus performance. Mr. Parker certainly isn't going to be happy if there's any delay in the circus!"

"But what about you?" Andie asked, obviously reluctant to leave her housemate.

"I'll stay with her," Ben said. "Milo, you make sure Andie gets to the dressing room. Rosalyn and I will meet you after the performance."

No one questioned his right to take charge. Milo simply nodded and took Andie's arm. With one last worried look at Rosalyn and Ben, Andie allowed herself to be led away.

Ben glanced around the area and noted that the crowd had dispersed. Even Parker had disappeared; he was probably already calling his insurance company. A few teenagers hung around, watching the fire fighters work, and the tattooed cowboy who'd bumped Ben earlier was now making a nuisance of himself in his efforts to help the emergency crews.

"Do you still feel the guy nearby?" he asked Rosalyn impulsively.

She shook her head. "The feelings are gone. I'm not picking up anything now. He could still be in the park . . . or he could be gone."

"Damn."

Rosalyn looked up at him with sympathetic under-
standing eyes. "This is all very frustrating for you, isn't
it, Benjamin?"

"Yeah. You could say that."

"You don't like uncertainties. You want neat logical
easily proven facts and conclusions. That's why you
like your work so much. You enjoy solving puzzles,
filling in blanks, seeing the truth come out and justice
done."

Ben shifted uncomfortably. "I don't think this is really the time for character analysis, do you?"

"Just making an observation," she said with a faint
smile.

Seeing that the emergency crews had finished their
work, Ben moved toward the blackened shell of the
tent. "Stay close to me," he told Rosalyn, determined
not to let her out of his sight. "I want to make a few ob-
servations of my own."

ANDIE SEEMED unusually distracted that evening. Ben
and Rosalyn tried to pull her into their dinner conversation, but her responses were little more than mono-
syllables. It was only after they'd cleaned the kitchen
and moved into the living room that she brought up the
topic that had been bothering her.

"Rosalyn?"

"Yes, Andie?"

"You said you sensed him there today?" It wasn't
necessary for her to be more specific about the "him."

Rosalyn nodded gravely. "He was there. He set the fire."

"With gasoline he'd brought into the park in a beer bottle," Ben added, revealing the results of his own investigation.

"Do you think he was trying to kill you today, or was this another warning?" Andie asked her friend.

"Another warning, I think," the older woman answered, her slight hesitation revealing her uncertainty.

"Probably," Ben concurred. "If he'd wanted anyone to die in that fire, it would have been fairly easy for him to arrange an explosion. As it was, the smoke gave everyone plenty of time to clear out."

Andie bit her lip. "So he's still toying with us."

"Looks that way," Ben said grimly. *And if I ever get my hands on the bastard . . .*

Rosalyn looked at him quickly. Ben cleared his throat and glanced away. Of course she couldn't actually read his mind, he reminded himself firmly, but sometimes she had a way of looking at him that made him wonder . . .

"What is he waiting for?" Andie asked in a sudden burst of words. She began to pace, her movements uncharacteristically jerky.

Ben reached out to her. "Andie . . ."

"He's waiting to catch me alone," Rosalyn said quietly. "He'll strike at the first opportunity now."

Ben and Andie turned to stare at her.

"How sure are you about that?" Ben asked reluctantly.

Rosalyn only looked at him.

"We have to leave here," Andie said, turning impulsively to Ben. "We have to go somewhere else, someplace where she'll be safe. We can't just keep waiting for him to make his move. The next time we might be too late to help her."

"Andie." Ben took her forearms and looked deeply into her frightened eyes. "We're *not* just sitting around waiting for him to make a move. And it would be foolish for us to act in panic at this point. For all we know, we could be playing right into his hands by doing so. I talked to a police investigator at the scene this afternoon, and he agreed that the best thing we can do is to stay on guard, watch for anything suspicious, call for help at the slightest indication of trouble. The guy isn't Superman. He's going to screw up, and when he does, we've got him."

"Shouldn't we hire some sort of security—like a bodyguard or something for Rosalyn? Maybe we should buy a gun."

"Rosalyn has had a bodyguard for the past three days," Ben told her calmly.

Andie's eyes widened. "But . . . who?"

"Tiny," he answered. "I told him the whole story. He's been within ten feet of the fortune-teller's tent while I kept an eye on you during working hours."

"Then how . . . ?"

"Tiny went to the bathroom," Ben explained with a sigh. "He let his guard down for just a few minutes and the jerk struck."

Andie whipped her head around to look at Rosalyn. "You knew about this?"

"I didn't tell her," Ben admitted. "I thought it would make her uncomfortable to know someone was watching her that closely."

"I knew," Rosalyn said with a smile. "I thought it was very sweet actually."

Ben scowled, but let it go. "As for the gun—I've got one."

Andie stared at him. "You do?"

"It's stashed in your bedroom—in the drawer you cleared out for my things. I'm hoping I won't be needing it, but I'm taking precautions, Andie. I haven't taken your safety—or Rosalyn's—for granted."

She sighed and touched his face. "I'm sorry. I know you're doing everything you can. I guess the tension is getting to me."

"That's understandable," he murmured, tugging her into his arms for a hug. "It's getting to all of us."

Andie rested against his shoulder for a moment, then pulled away, pushing a dark curl from her face. "Blake has a tattoo," she said, her voice very quiet.

Ben froze at the unexpected comment. "He what?"

"A tattoo," she repeated. "On his right wrist. I saw it this afternoon just before he buttoned his sleeve. I didn't think you'd seen it."

"No, I didn't." Ben whirled to face Rosalyn, who looked as startled as he felt. "What about Blake? Have you sensed anything about him?"

"Nothing," she answered with a shake of her head. "There are some people I simply can't read, no matter how hard I try. Blake is one of them."

"He doesn't frighten you? Make you uneasy?"

"He never has," Rosalyn answered with a slight shrug. "But that doesn't mean it's impossible for him to be . . ."

"Damn." Ben ran a hand through his hair, thinking of the bits of information Rosalyn had given them about the stalker. Blake fit many of them. "I need a last name for this guy, some kind of background on him. How can I get it?"

"Mr. Parker is very insistent about the confidentiality of all personnel records," Andie said. "I don't think he'd let you look at any of the files."

"Chances are the guy lied on his job application, anyway," Ben muttered, rubbing a hand over his chin. "Do either of you know where he lives?"

Andie and Rosalyn exchanged glances, then looked back at Ben, shaking their heads.

It wasn't going to be easy to provide bodyguard service *and* conduct an investigation. Ben decided he'd give the matter some thought overnight, hoping he'd have some sort of plan formulated by morning. He hadn't been doing a lot of sleeping lately, anyway.

BLAKE DIDN'T SHOW UP for work at the park the next day. Everyone told Ben it was the first day Blake had missed since taking the job a month earlier. Ben asked several of Blake's associates if they knew where he lived;

no one did. Everyone liked the guy well enough, but no one seemed to really know him.

Frustrated, Ben watched over Andie and wished he could figure out a way to track Blake down. He felt Rosalyn was safe enough in Tiny's care; the big man had been deeply chagrined about the fire and had sworn to Ben he wouldn't let his guard down again. But there was no one short of his own brother Ben would have trusted with Andie's safety.

He wished Jonathan could be here to give him a hand, and he knew it would take only a telephone call to have Jon on a plane. But Ben wouldn't take his brother away from his family now. One way or another, he would handle this mess himself.

He just wished he knew what his next step should be.

MILO JOINED THEM for dinner that evening. They were all in fairly good spirits, since there had been no unpleasant incidents at the park that day. Rosalyn had been given temporary work quarters in a snug little trailer owned by the park, and the remains of the old tent were being cleared so that a new one could be erected. Parker had promised a more fireproof structure this time and had started investigating other potential fire hazards within the park, stating emphatically that fires "just weren't good for business."

"You have to admit it was pretty funny when the monkey got away from the clown during the circus performance," Ben said as they finished dessert. "The crowd loved it when he climbed the bleachers and grabbed the bag of peanuts from the hawker's tray."

Andie laughed, but shook her head. "Still, it could have been a disaster," she said. "If the monkey had bitten someone, we'd have had a lawsuit."

"Or the creature could have pooped on an expensive silk blouse and we'd have been sued for damages and emotional trauma," Milo added gravely. "You never know what will lead to a lawsuit against an amusement park."

"Like that guy who tried to sue earlier this year because he threw up on the roller coaster," Andie added with an expression of disgust.

Ben looked at her, puzzled.

"Public humiliation," she explained. "He thought the park should have been more specific in warning people that overdoses of junk food along with stomach-twisting rides can lead to embarrassing consequences."

"A real genius, wasn't he?" Ben said dryly.

Andie made a face. "That was one of the frivolous claims that didn't go anywhere. The ones that really make me mad are the people who fake injuries hoping to make big money from the park's insurance. Some people will go to any extreme to avoid honest work."

"Have you forgotten I investigate claims like that for a living? You wouldn't believe some of the wild stories I've heard or—"

The doorbell rang. "Anyone expecting company?" Ben asked.

Andie and Rosalyn shook their heads.

Ben rose. "I'll get it."

Andie was right behind him as he walked into the living room. It was she who gasped at the sight of their visitor. "Donald! What are you doing here?"

Her brother-in-law entered the room with an expression that made it quite clear what he thought of Andie's very modest home. "Hello, Andie. Luck. I'm surprised to see *you* here. I understand you checked out of your hotel room several days ago."

"I made arrangements for other accommodations," Ben answered smoothly. "You haven't answered Andie's question, Humphries. What *are* you doing here?"

"I realized it was time I did something about this myself," Donald answered stiffly. "We had hoped you would be successful in convincing Andie to return home, but either you've met with refusal or haven't tried hard enough."

"I never said I'd try to talk her into coming home," Ben reminded him. "I only promised to make sure she's okay."

"Donald, it really wasn't necessary for you to come all the way to Texas," Andie said, her hands propped on her hips. "I'm not coming back to Seattle—other than for an occasional visit with the family, of course. You might as well accept that and convince the others it's true. I'm happy here. I'm doing what I want to do. I just wish all of you would give me the freedom to make my own decisions."

"Is it true you're working as a circus clown?" Donald demanded, making the job sound roughly equivalent to "prostitute."

"Yes, I am," Andie said with a proud lift of her chin. She glared at Ben. "I guess you told him every detail of my life here?"

"No, I didn't," Ben protested. "I only told your family that you were in good health and seemed happy."

"I hired another investigator," Donald admitted. "The same day your parents contacted Luck. Once your grandmother revealed where you were living and working, the rest was easy enough to discover."

"Then why the hell did you send *me* down here?" Ben demanded, furious that Humphries had gone behind his back this way. "And who the hell is this other guy you hired? Has he been hanging around watching Andie?"

"Donald, how could you!" Andie said, eyes sparking with the temper that was now familiar to Ben.

Humphries held up both hands. "No one's been spying on you, Andie," he assured her, speaking as he probably would to a frightened child in his dental office. "It was all done by telephone. My man never left Seattle. I thought I'd give Luck a chance to talk to you and then take over myself if he met with refusal."

"Take over yourself?" Andie repeated, her eyes growing even darker.

Seeing the signs of an imminent eruption, Ben decided to keep quiet—for now. He figured Andie could handle this herself. He'd have his own little talk with Humphries later.

Apparently oblivious to Andie's mounting temper, Donald looked past her. "Who are these people?"

Rosalyn stepped forward, her hand outstretched. "I'm Andie's housemate, Rosalyn Carmody. This is our friend, Milo. And you are . . ."

"Dr. Humphries," Donald answered pompously. "Andie's brother-in-law."

Ben watched as Humphries took Rosalyn's offered hand. He bit the inside of his lip against a smile when an odd expression crossed the dentist's face.

"Hmm." Rosalyn studied the man with her intently searching violet eyes. "You're a very good dentist. You enjoy your work."

"Uh, yes, I do. Er—?"

"And you're quite fond of your wife."

Humphries was looking decidedly beleaguered now, as though wondering how to get himself out of this situation graciously. "Yes, of course I'm fond of my wife. Excuse me, but—"

Rosalyn's smile hardened. "It would be a shame for you to risk jeopardizing your marriage for a fling with your new receptionist, don't you agree, Doctor? I realize she's encouraging you, but do you really think it's worth taking that chance?"

Humphries's jaw dropped.

Andie drew herself even taller, her eyes snapping fire. "Donald! Don't you *dare* cheat on my sister!"

Donald dropped the psychic's hand as though he'd been burned and turned hastily to Andie. "Look, I don't know what this woman is talking about. I've never laid a hand on Caroline!"

"See that you don't," Andie replied curtly.

Ben took one look at Rosalyn's smug expression and had to hide a smile behind his hand.

"Now, Andie, it's obvious you've been having some emotional problems lately," her brother-in-law said as he made an attempt to reclaim his dignity. "Perhaps those of us who care about you missed seeing the warning signs. We should have been there for you sooner. But I promise you, if you'll just come home with me now, we'll see that you get help."

"That does it." Andie stalked to the door and flung it open. "Get out. Now."

"You can't be serious."

"I'm entirely serious. I want you out of my house. Tell my family that I send my love and I'll try to make it home for a brief visit when it's convenient for me to do so, but I have no intention of moving back. As for you, you pompous ass, I'm telling you right now to stay out of my business. And if you do anything to hurt my sister, I'll personally see to it that your precious reputation is dragged through the Seattle mud. Is that clear?"

Donald was clearly stunned. "Andie! I've never heard you talk this way."

"It won't be the last time," she told him. "Goodbye, Donald. Have a nice flight home."

"But I hired a cab to bring me here from the airport," he whined. "How will I get back?"

"I'll drive you," Ben volunteered promptly, seeing his chance to have his own little chat with the representative from Andie's overprotective family. "Milo, you'll stay with Rosalyn and Andie until I return, won't you?"

"Of course," Milo agreed with a smile. "Perhaps we'll play a few hands of cards. Andie's quite good at poker."

"Poker! She doesn't know how to play poker."

"Nonsense. She won two dollars from me just a week ago at penny ante," Milo informed Donald. "Perhaps we'll raise the stakes to a nickel tonight. Throw caution to the wind, so to speak."

Donald shook his head. "Andie, keep in mind that your family will always be there for you when you're ready to—"

"Goodbye, Donald." Andie's voice held no hesitation whatever.

He sighed deeply and turned toward the door.

Ben quickly brushed his mouth across Andie's. "I'll be back soon," he murmured. "Keep the door locked."

Still bristling from her confrontation with Donald, Andie nodded coolly. "I'm quite capable of taking adequate precautions."

He winced comically. "Oops. Sorry. Of course you are."

He could hear her foot still tapping against the hardwood floor as he closed the front door behind himself and her uninvited guest.

IT TOOK Andie more than half an hour and several hands of poker before she finally had her temper fully back under control.

"Feeling better, dear?" Rosalyn asked, smiling at her from across the kitchen table.

Andie nodded and scooped up the stack of pennies she'd just taken with a full house. "Much better, thank you. Your deal, Milo."

"Your brother-in-law really isn't a bad man," Rosalyn said. "He's genuinely concerned about you. He's just a bit stuffy."

"More than a bit. The man could serve as a walking advertisement for a taxidermist," Andie muttered. And then she cocked her head and asked, "Has he really been playing around on my sister? Because, if he has—"

"Calm down, Andie. He hasn't cheated on your sister. He has been tempted lately, but I'm not sure he'd have ever had the courage to do anything about it. Now that he's been confronted with his weakness, I doubt he'll even consider the possibility again. He really wouldn't want to hurt his marriage."

Slightly mollified, Andie nodded. "Good."

"It was a bit naughty of you to embarrass him that way in front of us," Milo told Rosalyn, though he was smiling as he spoke. "I've rarely seen such a stunned expression."

"I know I was bad, but I didn't like the way he spoke to Andie," Rosalyn admitted.

"You were wonderful." Andie smiled at the memory of Donald's shock, then glanced at her watch. "I wonder how much longer Ben will be."

"They're probably just now arriving at the airport," Milo replied, looking at his own vintage wristwatch. "I'd say it will be at least another hour before he returns."

"I hate for you to be out so late," Andie fretted, noticing the signs of weariness in Milo's face. He'd been up early that morning practicing a new illusion, and she was willing to bet he hadn't slept well since he'd learned about Rosalyn's problems. Milo needed his rest. "Why don't you go on home? We'll be fine for an hour or so, won't we, Rosalyn?"

Rosalyn, too, was studying Milo's face. "Of course we will. Do go home and rest, Milo. We'll see you in the morning."

Milo shook his balding head. "Absolutely not. I told Ben I would stay with you and that's exactly what I'm going to do. Now, ante up."

Andie squirmed in her hard little café chair and bit her lip to prevent herself from arguing with him. She certainly didn't want to hurt his pride by suggesting he would be of little help to them if something *did* happen. Darn Ben for making Milo feel as though it was his duty to play bodyguard for the evening!

"It won't do a bit of good to argue with him, Andie," Rosalyn said with a fond smile at Milo. "The man can be as stubborn as a mule. I suppose we should just go on with our game."

Andie conceded defeat. She picked up her cards, studied them, then winced. "You haven't been practicing card tricks, by any chance?" she demanded of Milo, her voice exaggeratedly suspicious. "Dealing off the bottom, perhaps?"

He looked suitably outraged. "Of course not! If you have a poor hand, it's simply the luck of the draw."

"Bad luck of the draw, you mean," Andie muttered, tossing a penny into the center of the table. "I'll take three cards."

"And I'll have—"

In a crash of splintered wood, the rather flimsy back door burst open.

A man with a gun in his hand stood in the doorway. He smiled with an evil intent that made Andie's blood run cold.

*Ben. Oh, Ben, where are you?*

IT WAS a forty-five-minute drive to the airport. Ben said little during the trip, but he was satisfied afterward that Andie's brother-in-law would leave her alone—for now at least. Donald still wasn't convinced that Andie hadn't suffered an emotional breakdown of some sort, but he seemed content with the knowledge that Ben's intentions were entirely honorable.

"At least you're from a decent family," Donald muttered. "It will make her family feel better to know there's someone watching out for her."

"You still don't get it, do you?" Ben asked with a disgusted shake of his head. "Andie doesn't need me—or anyone else—watching out for her. She wants those she cares about to accept her as she is, to encourage her independent spirit, not to stifle it."

He thought of Andie's fierce determination to protect her friend and wondered if she'd ever feel as loyally committed to him. God, he hoped so.

He wasn't sure how Andie felt about him actually, and he found the uncertainty frustrating. He suspected that Rosalyn had been right on target with her impromptu personality analysis. He liked his loose ends tied up, his puzzles neatly solved, his questions answered. And now he wanted—needed—to know Andie's feelings.

There'd been little time for them to discuss their developing relationship of course. She responded to his lovemaking with an eager intensity that took his breath away, but she'd never told him she loved him. Did she? Could she make love to him like that and not care as deeply as he did?

Benjamin Luck wasn't accustomed to self-doubts. He didn't much care for the idea that Andie might not want him as badly as he wanted her. And, Andie had realized early in their acquaintance, he hated to lose.

HE SPOTTED the movement outside the little rental house from half a block away. Acting instinctively, he jerked the car to the side of the road, turned off the lights and killed the engine. He would walk the rest of the way.

A man was crouched beside the front porch, a dark shape barely distinguishable in the shadows. Ben moved silently forward, but some sixth sense must have warned the guy he was near. He turned just as Ben made a flying leap forward. The trespasser hit the ground with a muted "oomph" of surprise.

With his captive pinned with one arm, Ben raised his fist, fully intending to smash the guy's face. A glimmer of light from one of the windows provided just enough illumination for Ben to identify the other man.

Blake.

"Now why doesn't this surprise me?" he growled, his fist tightening.

"You're making a mistake," Blake said, his voice strained from the pressure of Ben's arm across his throat. "I'm not the guy you're after. And I think something may be going on inside."

"Right," Ben muttered, disgusted at what seemed to be an obvious attempt to distract him. "I suppose you have a perfectly reasonable excuse for being here."

"I was watching the house," Blake admitted, still keeping his voice low. "I think someone's inside. I heard a crash. I was just going around to investigate when you tackled me."

Damn. The guy sounded sincere. Torn, Ben looked from the quiet house back down to the unresisting man beneath him. "Why would you be watching the house?"

"Would you quit playing Dick Tracy and see what's going on in there? They could be in danger. *Andie* could be in danger," Blake said, pushing against Ben's arm.

Ben hesitated only a moment longer, then muttered a curse and let Blake go. He was acting strictly on instinct, and that made him nervous. "If you're lying to me . . ." he said, and he made sure his deadly sincerity came through the warning.

"Trust me," Blake said with a quick slashing smile. And then he turned toward the house, leaving Ben to follow with some misgiving.

# 12

THE ARMED INTRUDER was of average height and weight, fair skinned and light haired. His face was marked with the scars of youthful acne, and his thin mouth seemed to be frozen in a permanent sneer. He wore a long-sleeved dark-colored shirt, but Andie knew that somewhere beneath it was a tattoo.

She knew she'd seen him at the park. It took her a moment, but then she recognized him as the biker she'd stumbled into and whose angry outburst had gotten him forcibly escorted from the park.

Now he was looking at Rosalyn with so much hatred in his pale eyes that Andie shivered. "It's eleven p.m., the eleventh of July," he said, his voice oddly shrill. "I've been waiting for this time."

Rosalyn sat very still. "Yes," she said, and her own tone was surprisingly calm. "I know you have."

"You don't *know* anything!" the gunman shouted, suddenly infuriated. "It's all bullshit! A scam. You don't read minds. You can't predict the future. You didn't even know I've been standing outside your house for the past half-hour waiting for the right time. You're a fake, lady. And I hate fakes."

"If you're so convinced I'm a fake, then why do I frighten you so much?" Rosalyn asked logically.

"You don't scare me."

"Don't I, Frank?"

His eyes widened, then narrowed. "How did you know my name?"

Rosalyn only smiled. "You tell me."

"Stop it!" he yelled again, making Andie jump. "Just stop it, you hear? I hate that psychic crap."

*Think, Andie. You've been telling everyone you can take care of yourself. Now do something, dammit.* But she couldn't think of anything to do, except to sit very still and pray that an opportunity for rescue would present itself.

The gunman suddenly froze. "What was that?"

"I didn't hear anything," Milo said, looking around the tiny kitchen and blinking his eyes as though he wasn't quite sure what was happening. He looked very much like an old, confused little man. Andie was well aware that Milo was deliberately projecting that image.

"Shut up." Frank cocked his head, his eyes blank as he listened for whatever had caught his attention. "Sounded like it came from outside. Around front," he muttered.

*Ben?* Andie clenched her hands in her lap, hoping it was Ben and just as deeply afraid that it was.

"What are you going to do to us?" Rosalyn asked, and Andie wondered if she was deliberately trying to distract him from the noise. Did Rosalyn, too, suspect that Ben was outside? Or did she *know* he was?

"You and the old man are going to die," Frank answered Rosalyn with a chilling smile of anticipation.

He glanced at Andie, and she shuddered at what she saw in his eyes. "You," he murmured, moving closer, "will live a little longer than the others. But then you'll join them."

Andie lifted her chin and forced herself to meet his gaze, refusing to show the sick fear swirling inside her.

He laughed shortly and motioned with the gun. "Everyone on your feet," he said. "No sudden moves. Don't try anything stupid."

Andie and Rosalyn rose very slowly. Milo followed, though he stumbled as he got to his feet. His face was pale, shiny with sweat.

Frank trained the gun on him. "What's wrong with you, old man? Can't you even stand up?"

Milo's right hand was on his chest and he was breathing in short loud gulps. "My . . . my heart," he gasped, fumbling at his breast pocket. "I can't—"

"Milo?" Rosalyn took a quick step toward him. Andie's hands tightened on the back of her chair. She stared at Milo, unable to tell whether his distress was real or feigned.

"Don't move!" Frank barked, turning the gun on Rosalyn. His finger tightened on the trigger.

It happened very quickly. Andie saw Milo's hand move, and then there was a muffled explosion and a blinding flash of light only a couple of feet from Frank. Frank jerked violently, clearly disoriented. Rosalyn screamed, either from genuine fear or to add to the confusion.

Andie acted on instinct. She picked up her chair and swung it with every ounce of her strength at the back of Frank's head. The chair hit him across the neck and shoulders with enough impact to jar Andie all the way to her toes.

Frank stumbled. The gun went off. Out of the corner of her eye, Andie saw Milo and Rosalyn both drop, but she took no time to check on them. She swung the chair again.

Frank went down that time. The gun clattered against the floor.

Two figures suddenly appeared in the shattered doorway. "Andie!" Ben shouted.

She dropped the chair and ran into his arms.

There was a brief vicious struggle, Frank's head hit the floor with a sickening thud. This time he didn't move.

Blake looked up in grim satisfaction. "Someone call the cops," he said. "And get me something to tie this guy up with."

Andie was too dazed even to wonder what Blake was doing there. "Rosalyn?" she said, pulling reluctantly out of Ben's strong arms. "Milo?"

Rosalyn was kneeling on the floor beside Milo. "We're fine, dear," she said. "I believe Milo has twisted his ankle, but other than that we're uninjured."

"Thank God," Andie whispered, then had to fight back a sudden wave of tears. She shook her head when

Ben reached out to her and turned toward the telephone. She needed to do something to ward off the hysteria that was threatening to overtake her.

MILO WAS A HERO. He sat in a deep armchair, sipping hot tea, his bandaged swollen ankle propped on an ottoman. Andie and Rosalyn hovered over him admiringly. Finally he laughed and waved them back. "I'm fine," he assured them. "It's just a slight sprain. I don't need anything more to eat or to drink, no more pain pills and no more pillows for my back or ankle. But thank you."

"It was just so clever of you to throw that flashing thing," Rosalyn said. "Had you not startled him, someone might have been seriously injured before Ben and Blake could rescue us."

"You both knew they were out there, didn't you?" Andie asked, moving to sit on the arm of Ben's chair.

"I suspected someone was," Milo admitted. "Something about Rosalyn's expression gave me hope. I thought the three of us could duck out of range and give Ben a chance to rush the guy. I didn't expect you to start swinging your chair," he added with a chiding look at Andie.

Rosalyn interceded. "I knew Ben was outside," she said with a slight frown. "I sensed someone with him, but I wasn't sure who it was. I simply can't read Blake, no matter how hard I try."

All eyes turned to Blake, who lounged comfortably on the couch and sipped a cold beer.

"Speaking of Blake," Ben murmured, leaning forward in his chair and pinning the other man with a frown. "Who the hell *are* you, anyway?"

Blake drained the last of the beer and set the bottle on the scarred coffee table in front of him. "I'm a PI," he said.

"A *what*?" Andie said with a startled gasp.

"A private investigator," he clarified.

"Who hired you?" Ben demanded.

Blake looked at Rosalyn as he answered. "Marie Mitchell's father."

An expression of deep sadness crossed Rosalyn's face. "Of course," she murmured. "That poor young woman."

"Who is she?" Andie asked.

Blake replied. "One of the bastard's victims. She died without regaining consciousness two days after he attacked her. Her father is a wealthy businessman and she was his only child. He was willing to spend every nickel he had to find the man who killed her."

"You followed him here? You knew who he was?" Ben asked.

Blake shook his head. "Rosalyn was my lead," he explained. "She'd come the closest to identifying him, and he'd found her twice before. I figured if I kept an eye on her long enough, he'd eventually show up."

"You were using her as bait!" Andie said indignantly.

"In a way," Blake agreed. He looked apologetically at Rosalyn. "But I was also hoping to protect you. I've been watching you as closely as possible. It helped that I was able to get a job at the park—the juggling I picked up as a kid finally came in handy."

"Why didn't you tell someone who you really were?" Milo asked, puzzled.

Blake shrugged. "I tend to work alone. And I wasn't sure who could be trusted." He glanced at Ben. "For a while, I thought you might be the guy I was after—especially when I found out you were using a fake identity. Once you told Andie who you really were, I checked you out and decided you were okay."

"Big of you," Ben muttered. "I thought it was you, of course."

Blake grinned, well aware that Ben was feeling disgruntled by his rather secondary role in the big rescue. Andie patted Ben's hand. "You've been wonderful to Rosalyn and me," she assured him. "You've spent hours guarding us and making sure we were safe. No one could have done more."

"I wasn't the one swinging the chair tonight," he reminded her, his eyes softening as he looked up at her. "You really can take care of yourself, can't you, slugger?"

She smiled. "That's what I've been trying to tell everyone."

"Remind me not to make you mad when there's furniture around."

She laughed, then caught her breath when the look in his eyes changed from teasing to hungry. She knew exactly what he would have liked to be doing right then.

Her own body, stimulated by the action and tense from adrenaline, tightened in similar need.

Blake rose in one fluid motion. "It's late," he said. "I've got a plane to catch in the morning. Guess I'd better be going."

"You're leaving Texas?" Andie asked quickly.

He nodded. "This job's done. Time to collect my pay and move on."

She realized she would miss him. She rose and offered him her hand. "You've been a good friend," she told him. "Thank you."

He smiled and lightly brushed his mouth across her cheek. "You take care of yourself, kid. Don't let anyone push you around, you hear?"

"I won't," she promised.

Blake turned to Ben, who'd also risen. He held out his hand. "We'd have made a pretty good team, I think."

Ben grimaced, though he took the offered hand in a firm grip. "We would have if you'd told me what the hell was going on."

Blake shrugged. "When the chips were down, you came through. Thanks for not choking me when you had the chance."

After exchanging warm farewells with Rosalyn and Milo, Blake took his leave. Andie could hear the faint whistled strains of a Disney tune in his wake.

Rosalyn insisted that Milo stay the night, saying with a faint blush that he could stay in her room. "So that I can keep an eye on that ankle," she added nonchalantly.

Andie bit down on her lower lip to prevent a smug grin from spreading across her face. She turned to Ben. "Since you don't have a hotel room to go to, you might as well stay, too," she said flippantly. "I could probably make room for you somewhere."

He grinned. "I'd appreciate that."

Andie and Rosalyn didn't quite meet each other's eyes as they bade each other good-night and hustled their men to the bedrooms.

SOMETIME IN THE NIGHT, Andie awoke shivering in delayed reaction. Ben drew her into his arms, murmuring reassurances. He called her a true heroine, praised her for her quick thinking and fast reflexes, told her how much he admired her, how deeply he cared for her, how badly he wanted her.

Andie brought the words to an end by pressing her mouth to his. Even after the passionate lovemaking they'd shared only hours before, she was suddenly consumed with need for him. Perhaps as an affirmation that they were alive, and whole, and safe. And together.

At least for tonight, she thought wistfully, and wrapped her legs tightly around his warm lean hips as he slipped easily into her.

ANDIE THE CLOWN basked in the innocent laughter of a pigtailed little girl and waved goodbye as the child was escorted away by her smiling parents. It was another relentlessly hot day, but Andie didn't mind the weight of her bright wig or the tight feel of the heavy makeup on her face. She twitched her nose, just to feel the tickle of the red foam ball.

She was happy. She was free. She and her friends were safe. She was doing exactly what she wanted to be doing. It would take only one more thing to make her life perfect.

"Hi, clown. Got a balloon for me?"

She turned eagerly in response to the deep drawl. Ben smiled at her, his emerald eyes glowing in a way that made her shiver with warm memories. It had been exactly one week since she'd stumbled into his arms for the first time, she realized rather dazedly.

How could her life have changed so drastically in such a staggeringly short time?

Ben tapped a foot against the pavement, to bring her attention back to him. "Hello? Is there anyone inside all that makeup and costume?"

She grinned, the expression crinkling her caked cheeks. "I'll let you find that out for yourself—later," she promised in a low voice after making sure no children were close enough to hear the provocative comment.

His smile deepened. "I like the sound of that."

"So do I."

Two little boys rushed up to shake Andie's hand. She mugged for them for a moment and elicited a burst of giggles before they dashed off to ride the carousel.

"You're very good with children," Ben commented when they were alone again.

"Thank you. I love kids."

"Great. Let's have half a dozen or so of our own."

Andie stumbled over her size-thirteen shoes. Ben's hand shot out to steady her. "Uh...what did you say?" she asked, staring up at him.

"I want kids. Don't you?"

"Well, yes, but I—"

"And just to make everything nice and tidy, I suppose we'd better get married first. I'd like to do it soon. Do you mind a very short engagement? We'll stay in Texas, of course, if you like. I've grown quite fond of Mercury. Seems like a good place to start a family. Of course, my work will take me away quite a bit, but I'll keep the travel to a minimum as much as possible. And we both know you're quite capable of taking care of yourself while I'm away, so—"

"Married?" Andie interrupted the flow of words in a squeaky voice. "You want to get married?"

He was actually proposing to her? *Here? Now?*

His broad grin couldn't quite hide the hint of vulnerability in his eyes. "Yeah. I want to get married. I've never wanted anything more in my life. Unless it's too soon for you? We could always wait a while if you—"

She threw herself into his arms with a force that made him stagger. Her red foam nose fell unnoticed to the ground when she covered his mouth with her own. Ben's arms closed around her with a strength that told her he took her enthusiastic response for an acceptance of his proposal.

This was all that had been missing, she thought joyously. Now her life was perfect.

"I love you," Ben murmured the moment she drew back for a quick breath. "I love you. I—"

She kissed him again.

"Jackie, look! That man is kissing the clown."

"Eeww, gross! Clown's aren't supposed to kiss."

Andie pulled herself out of Ben's arms, suddenly conscious of their very public surroundings. One look at his face had her convulsed with laughter.

Ben watched her quizzically. "This isn't the way you're supposed to react when you've just gotten engaged."

"I know," she managed to say, "but . . ." She pointed at his face and broke into a fresh round of giggles.

Frowning, he touched his cheek. His fingers came away streaked with white and red paint. He grimaced. "How bad is it?"

"Let's just say we could almost pass as twins at the moment," she replied, patting his smeared face with one gloved hand. "Come on, darling. I'll show you how to take that stuff off."

"You do know how to entice a guy," Ben murmured, sliding an arm around her waist as they headed toward the employee dressing rooms. "Oh, and by the way, isn't there something you've neglected?"

She looked up at him with a blissful smile. "I love you, Benjamin Luck."

His arm tightened around her. His voice became husky. "That's exactly what I needed to hear."

# Epilogue

THE COUNTRY CLUB ballroom was crowded with an interesting assortment of guests. Andie's family stood clustered in one corner of the room, trying without much success to prevent themselves from staring at some of her more eccentric friends.

Looking utterly stunning in foaming white lace that contrasted beautifully with her dark hair and eyes, Andie worked her way through the room, thanking each guest for attending, looking as happy as Ben had ever seen her. He watched her with love and pride. *My wife*, he thought, still rather dazed at the reality. *Hot damn.*

"Congratulations, little brother," Jonathan Luck said, handing Ben a glass of champagne. "I heartily approve of your choice."

"She is special, isn't she?"

Jon nodded, then glanced across the room to where his own wife stood beside her neatly groomed nephew. Amanda Luck cradled baby Katherine in her arms as she chatted with her in-laws, who seemed much more comfortable in the eclectic gathering than the McBride family. "I'd say we both did quite well for ourselves," Jon murmured.

"I'd say you're right," Ben agreed. They tipped their champagne glasses in celebration of their marital contentment.

Rosalyn approached the brothers with a glowing smile. Milo followed close behind her. Only the night before, Milo had happily confided to Ben that he'd finally found the courage to ask Rosalyn to marry him. Rosalyn had accepted, to Milo's delight and Ben's hearty approval.

"Ben," she said now, fondly patting his arm, "Andie is positively beaming. I couldn't be happier for the two of you."

Ben brushed a kiss across her soft cheek. He had come to realize that Rosalyn and Milo would be a permanent part of his life now, and he wasn't sorry. They were good friends. "Thanks, Rosalyn. I know you and Milo will be as happy as Andie and I are."

Rosalyn turned to Jon, whom she'd met the day before. "I've just been admiring your new daughter," she said. "She's lovely."

"Thank you." Jon eyed her warily, as uncomfortable as Ben had been at first with an allegedly genuine psychic.

Rosalyn patted Jon's arm, much the same way she had Ben's. "You'll be a good father—to little Katherine and to the son you'll have next year," she assured him.

Jon's eyes widened comically.

Ben snickered.

Rosalyn turned with a mischievous smile. "As for you, Benjamin . . ."

Ben's smile abruptly faded. "What about me?"

Rosalyn chuckled. "It won't always be easy, being the father of beautiful twin daughters. But I have great confidence in you, my dear. You'll manage quite nicely."

Ben choked. *"Twins?"* he repeated. "Dammit, Rosalyn . . ."

But she only smiled and drifted away. Milo gave Ben a sympathetic pat on the shoulder before following his unusual fiancée.

"Ben?" Andie searched his face in concern as she approached him, clutching the full skirt of her gown to keep from tripping over it.

He knew his smile must be a rather sickly one. "Er . . . Andie? Do twins run in your family by any chance?"

"No. Why do you ask?"

And then her eyes widened and she looked quickly after Rosalyn. "Twins?" she said thickly. "Us?"

Ben nodded.

"Heavens," she said, and her voice was a bit weak. But then she looked up at him, and her smile took his breath away. "I think we can handle it, don't you?"

Ben reflected that there was nothing he couldn't handle as long as Andie McBride Luck was beside him, looking at him in just this way. "I'm sure we'll manage just fine," he promised her, and bent his head to kiss her loving happy smile.

# Look out for Temptation's bright, new, stylish covers...

### They're Terrifically Tempting!

We're sure you'll love the new raspberry-coloured Temptation books—our brand new look from December.

Temptation romances are still as passionate and fun-loving as ever and they're on sale now!

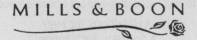

MILLS & BOON

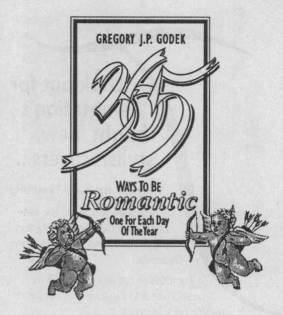

### GREGORY J.P. GODEK

## 365

### WAYS TO BE
### *Romantic*
#### One For Each Day Of The Year

## *A Book Designed to be Given…*

A collection of creative, unusual and wonderful ideas, to add a
spark to your relationship–and put a twinkle in your eye.

### A Handbook for Men
### A Godsend for Women

Why be romantic? Why bother?
Simple. It's inexpensive, easy–and lots of *fun*!

**Available January 1995**          Price: £4.99 (Hardback)

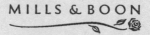

## MILLS & BOON

Available from selected bookshops and newsagents.

# PENNY JORDAN

## Cruel Legacy

*One man's untimely death deprives a wife of her husband, robs a man of his job and offers some-one else the chance of a lifetime...*

Suicide — the only way out for Andrew Ryecart, facing crippling debt. An end to his troubles, but for those he leaves behind the problems are just beginning, as the repercussions of this most desperate of acts reach out and touch the lives of six different people — changing them forever.

**Special large-format paperback edition**

**OCTOBER**       **£8.99**

## WORLDWIDE

This month's
irresistible novels from

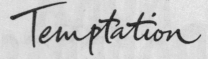

**WILD LIKE THE WIND by Janice Kaiser**

*Fire, Wind, Earth, Water—but nothing is more elemental than passion.*

Julia Powell believed she could live without passion. But she couldn't survive without her abducted daughter, Zara. She was willing to do whatever it took to get her back, including marrying a man she hardly knew—the notorious Cole Bonner...

**JOYRIDE by Leandra Logan**

Dan Burke was not looking forward to Christmas...until Joy Jones arrived on his doorstep, needing help. A second chance with Joy was what he had secretly dreamed of, but could Dan survive having his heart broken again?

**JUST HER LUCK by Gina Wilkins**

It was just Andie McBride's luck to be tracked down by a sinfully sexy man sent by her suffocating family. He might turn her into a mass of quivering desire, but he, too, was domineering. Had her luck run out?

**I'LL BE SEEING YOU by Kristine Rolofson**

After fifty years, destiny brought two wartime lovers back together. Destiny also brought Nicholas Ciminero and Sarah McGrath together, and it was as if they were made for each other. But were they destined to repeat the mistakes of the past?

Spoil yourself next month
with these four novels from

## AFTERSHOCK by Lynn Michaels

*Fire, Wind, Earth, Water—but nothing is more elemental than passion.*

Rockie Wexler's father had disappeared, and she needed some help rescuing him. It came in the shape of Leslie Sheridan—but didn't he have reasons for hating the Wexler name?

## LOVE POTION No. 9 by Kate Hoffmann

When Susannah invented a love potion, it seemed to work: handsome Jay Beaumont fell in love with her. But she'd never intended to fall in love with him...

## ANGEL OF DESIRE by JoAnn Ross

*Dreamscape Romance*

Rachel Parrish had to stop Shade's quest for vengeance. But she hadn't counted on her very *womanly* response to him. Because Rachel had been heaven-sent with no experience of earthly pleasures...

## LOVERBOY by Vicki Lewis Thompson

Luke Bannister, TV's sexiest star, was finally coming home. But childhood sweetheart Meg wasn't going to join his harem. He had dumped her once—she wasn't about to let it happen again!